THE FIRES OF AUTUMN

This is a work of fiction inspired by historical events that took place in Europe, early in the fourteenth century.

THE FIRES OF AUTUMN

RHONDA CHANDLER

STAIRCASE BOOKS

THE FIRES OF AUTUMN

Copyright © 2018, by Rhonda Chandler

www.rhondachandler.com

Cover Design and Layout by Kristen Langefeld with additional image from chuttersnap on Unsplash.

Map Creation and Design by Rhonda Chandler and Kristen Langefeld.

Scripture taken from the HOLY BIBLE, NEW INTERNATIONAL VERSION®

Copyright © 1973,1978,1984 by International Bible Society. Used by permission of Zondervan. All rights reserved.

ISBN 978-1-7325797-0-5 (paperback)

ISBN 978-1-7325797-1-2 (large print)

ISBN 978-1-7325797-2-9 (ebook)

Staircase Books

1111 S. Lincoln Ave. #465

O'Fallon, IL 62269-9998

~

*To all those who have difficulty
recognizing the faces of their sisters and brothers*

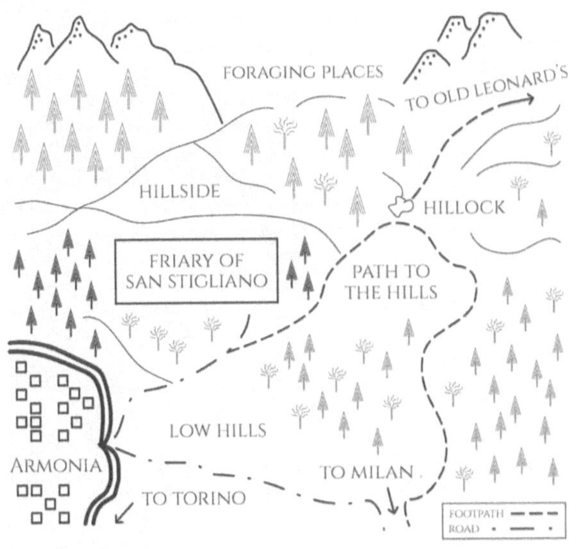

The Friary of San Stigliano

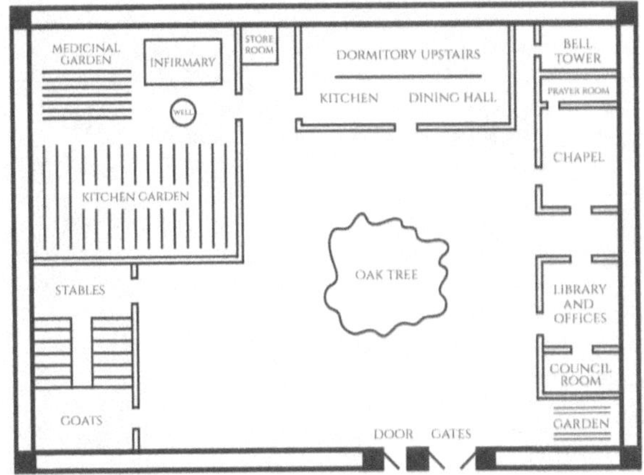

THE FRIARS OF SAN STIGLIANO
AT THE TIME OF THE TROUBLES, 1318
AMADEUS WALERIAN, Guardian
KERSTAN, lector, assistant to the Guardian
QUINTUS, physician
CANTOR, physician's assistant
EMILIAN
BENEFICE
FABRIZIO
GUSTAVE, Lay brother, cook and baker
Launderers and kitchen boys
DONATELLO, proxy procurator, Friary of San Stigliano
PRENTICE, scrivener
A small group of scriveners and scholars

THE VISITING FRANCISCANS
VENEDICTOS
SERENO
LUCIEN
PALMER
LAUDALINO
HONORATO

THE INQUISITOR'S PARTY
NOBILUS, Dominican friar, inquisitor
MANUS, civil servant
TITUS, Dominican friar
Assisting Dominican friars, servants, and grooms

List submitted by BROTHER KERSTAN

1

Fabrizio was sitting on the hillside with the goats, his back against a boulder, singing a psalm in the early September sunshine, when he saw the rising cloud of smoke. The song faltered in his mouth as he stared at the dirty-white mass lifting to the sky. The light breeze shifted, bringing with it the smell of smoldering wood and grass. The goats muttered nervously.

He climbed the boulder, squinting into the distance to make out the source of the smoke. But the folds of the hills hid it from him. The town did not lie in that direction. Neither did the mills that turned wool into yarn. What could be burning? A straggly, long-haired goat got to her feet and let out a bawl. Fabrizio jumped off the boulder, picked up his staff, and went to her.

"The fire is very far from us, Ermentrude," he said, rubbing her neck to calm her. "Still, you have been foraging on these slopes for several hours. We can start back down now." The goat leaned against him as he stroked her back, her long, gray coat blending with his long, gray friar's robe.

He called to the others. "Sancha! Lily! Bring your sisters!"

They bleated their protest at having their rest interrupted, but rose and trotted obediently toward him. Together, the small herd picked its way across the hillside and had just gained the main downward path, when Fabrizio heard someone calling his name.

A man was striding toward him across the sloping meadow, his peasant robe swirling around his knees, his legs covered and laced with soft leather, a broad, flat-brimmed hat on his head, his massive staff swinging out and striking the ground with every stride. It was Old Leonard, a wise, and therefore prosperous, peasant. He kept not goats, but sheep, a large, beautiful herd that Fabrizio could see scattered across the slopes behind him. The wool from these sheep went to the riverside mills and thence to the weavers in town. Some of Old Leonard's grown sons wandered among the well-protected flock.

As Old Leonard approached, he waved his arm angrily at the cloud of smoke. "Fabrizio, have you seen that? I think Antonio has gone crazy." Old Leonard planted his staff firmly in the ground when he stopped to talk. "He has to be the first to burn his fields so he can be the first to plant his winter farro."

"Burning his fields? Why would he want to do that?" Fabrizio asked.

Old Leonard snorted. "He picked up the idea from some stranger at the spring market in Torino. Claims that burning makes it faster to clear out all the stubble in the fields. The forest keeps sending seeds into them, and Antonio gets angry at all the short trees that spring up. Once he has harvested the farro, he says it's faster to burn the small trees rather than dig out each one."

Old Leonard gestured to indicate the farmland below them. "And, of course, if Antonio does it, everyone else will do it too, even if they don't have troublesome trees near their fields."

"But what would Antonio's lord say about it?"

The old man shook his head. "I can barely believe it, but Antonio convinced him first of all. They'll be burning their fields for weeks now that Antonio has started. All around us, smoke, smoke, smoke! I cannot help thinking that fire burns more than wood and stubble. I won't feel safe until the autumn is over and the winter stops this foolishness."

Fabrizio thought he would prefer the warmth of the fires to the coming cold of winter, but said nothing. Old Leonard, his anger spent for the moment, reached out to pet the goats. The herd immediately began to push towards him, eager to get their share of caresses from their friend. The old man laughed.

"What a herd you have, Fabrizio. I marvel every time I see it. Long-haired, short-haired, horns, no horns, brown, black, gray, white. Such a mix! You have two of one breed, three of another, these four here, this one there, and that one who should have horns but doesn't, and yet without her horns she still rules them all."

Ermentrude, the curiously hornless one, had stayed by Fabrizio's side. He stroked her head, smiling. "When your herd is made up of what you have been given, this is what it looks like."

He could not help but glance again at Old Leonard's

sheep. There were several hundred in that herd, each one a creamy white dot against the green grass. But Fabrizio wouldn't trade his goats for any amount of sheep.

He scratched Ermentrude under her chin, then reached out to rub Lily's back. "They are good girls with good hearts. Every spring they give their kids to poor families. Every day they give us milk to make cheese. I am very grateful to them and I love them all."

"Ah, there, there is your secret!" Old Leonard cried. "They should be tearing each other apart, and yet, they are not. Why? Because you love each one and they know it!" Sancha nuzzled up to Ermentrude, careful to keep her horns away. "Look how friendly this one is with that!"

They watched the goats in silence for a few moments. When the old man spoke again, his tone was serious.

"I want to thank you and your friary, Fabrizio, for letting my grandson help in the kitchen. His mother won't accept any help from me. I think she is ashamed of her slothful husband, yet she defends him." Old Leonard tugged slowly on his gray beard, his eyes still on the goats. "The money you pay Little Leo is all his mother gets some weeks."

"But the money does not come from us—" Fabrizio began.

"Yes, yes, I know," Old Leonard broke in. "Franciscans have no money, keep no money, and touch no money. I know it is Donatello your procurator who handles these things for you. But it is you Franciscans who have given Leo a place." The peasant pulled off his hat and scratched his head fiercely. "Pray to God he doesn't turn out like his father."

Fabrizio did not know what to say to this. He had never

seen his own father and had often wondered if he had grown to be like him in some way.

"I think young Leo tries very hard," he said. "He always does what Gustave tells him to do."

Old Leonard grunted, replaced his hat, and leaned on his staff again. "As he should," he replied. But he seemed pleased by the report.

The peasant turned his head to squint at the land around them and Fabrizio followed his gaze.

High above them, clouds hid the dark mountain peaks. Below them, the Lombardy hills rippled their way down to the river plain where sunshine reigned.

Between each roll of ground, small hamlets and farms tucked themselves in the hills' pockets. Meadows, woodland, and farmland displayed every shade of green and gold possible for the eye's delight. Standing on the slope as high as they did now, on a day when no low clouds obscured their view, they could see towns far distant, basking on sunny riversides. Fabrizio took a deep breath of pleasure at the beauty of it all.

"I should also tell you," said Old Leonard, "that Antonio, this fire-starter, is telling everyone to be watchful for wild dogs in the hills. That doesn't mean he has seen any himself, of course. But he loves very much to be the teller of things."

The pleasure turned to alarm. Fabrizio instinctively reached his hand out for Ermentrude. They rambled often in the hills, and occasionally came across mangled, torn carcasses of sheep, deer, and forest animals. Once he saw a half-eaten goat. He always wondered who the animals were and who might be missing them.

Such sights cut him to the heart and made him grateful

for the staff Old Leonard had given him several years ago. But it had been some time since he had seen the remains of torn beasts. He shook his head.

"I have seen no dogs. All has been peaceful for days."

"We may never see the dogs, Fabrizio. Antonio likes to scare people, to see their wide eyes and hear their gasps at something he has said. Still," Old Leonard cast a glance back at his sheep, "we must always be careful." Having made this pronouncement, he hunched over, leaning on his staff, thinking. Fabrizio waited until the old man straightened abruptly and took his staff in hand again.

"That's it! That's what I wanted to tell you. I was in town yesterday and there were some poor-looking friars in the streets begging for food. At first, I thought they had come from your friary, but I didn't know any of their faces. Their robes were torn and frayed. They looked almost wild. I had bread in my bag so I gave it to them. What is that proverb your Brother Benefice likes to say?"

"He says many," Fabrizio replied. "His head is filled with them."

"I don't know much Latin. Don't need it with the sheep. But it starts with *Occurrit*... No. I won't try to be above my place. Here's how I know it. 'God meets every man, but few recognize Him.' That's why I gave them the bread. Do you know anything about these friars?"

Fabrizio felt that he should know about them, but couldn't think of why. Sometimes he didn't pay as much attention to the news and events that took place in his Order as he ought. He shook his head. "No, I don't know, but I am usually in the friary or up here with the goats."

"They claimed they were Franciscans, so I thought you

might know." Old Leonard was clearly hoping for knowledge Fabrizio didn't have.

Fabrizio smiled. "For a hundred years now there have been Franciscans, moving all over the world. I know very few of them. Not many beyond those in the friary walls and some in Milan."

Old Leonard nodded. "I thought they might be lying. Saying they were Franciscans just to get food. But when I saw how poor they really were, I thought, lying or not, Fabrizio would feed them anyway." He gave a broad smile.

Fabrizio took the smile to heart. "Thank you, kind sir. I'm glad you thought of that."

Old Leonard drew himself up and put on a pompous face. "Oh, 'Sir?' I'm 'Sir' now?" He winked at Fabrizio. "Let's save that for Donatello's father! The man who truly owns all these sheep!"

With a nod of farewell, the old man turned and headed toward his herds and his own business.

Fabrizio called after him. "I will keep a look out for any sign of the wild dogs."

The peasant waved in response as he strode away.

THE MEMORIES OF TORN ANIMALS, nevertheless, made Fabrizio urge the goats down the hillside faster than usual. They bleated and bawled from time to time, but followed him steadily down the steep path.

"I cannot help it, sisters," he called out. "As our friend said, we must be watchful!"

He slowed his steps with relief when he caught sight of

the friary's red-stoned campanile. It was beautiful, this square tower, with an arched opening on each of its sides and a single gracious bell to peal the hours. The lovely notes often rang across the hillsides settling down into Armonia, the hard-working little town below them. To Fabrizio, each peal was the sound of peace, of home, of a place to live and work and belong, a mark of the security of his life as a Franciscan, and the healing of all that had come before. He paused for a moment, took a deep breath and let out a sigh of contentment.

Years ago, as a postulant, he had been sent to Milan, and though he had delighted in becoming a Franciscan, he also feared that he would be stuck in that great city, or, worse yet, sent elsewhere, even far away from the friary that had sheltered him. When he had been sent back to San Stigliano to be part of its mission, his joy was complete.

He led his herd down the familiar hillside paths and soon the rest of the red-tiled roofs came into view—the chapel; the dormitory; the infirmary; the library; the walls surrounding the garden plots with their orderly rows of onions, carrots, beans, greens, and medicinal herbs. There was the roof of the stables, originally built for a nobleman's proud collection of fine horses. Now half of it remained mostly empty, used only for Donatello's lonely horse and that of his bored groom.

The other half of the stables was home to the treasured goats of San Stigliano. Under Fabrizio's care, their milk produced an incredibly fine cheese. This cheese was one of the friary's main sources of food and a blessing to the poor who regularly came to ease their hunger at the friary's board. But it was Gustave, a lay brother, who actually made the cheese using his mother's recipe.

All the brothers contributed to the life of the friary and to the lives of the people outside it who needed them. Emilian taught the poor town boys how to make shoes, tailor clothes, and do all sorts of practical things. Benefice's chickens laid many eggs, while he collected proverbs, played the flute, rang the bell, and brought music to the hopeless. Cantor helped Quintus in tending the sick. Kerstan, alongside their Guardian, preached and taught and encouraged both friars and townspeople. All the friar brothers worked in the gardens and did every needed task. And every one of them spoke of the salvation of God as they worked and prayed among the people.

Fabrizio continued downward, his rope sandals finding secure footholds on the rough path. The goats, led by Ermentrude, moved dutifully along after him, Lily, ever watchful, at the end of the line. The psalm that he had enjoyed in the hills came to him again, and he began to sing it. Not to himself. To the Lord of Heaven, who in His mercy had made a home and a true family for a lost boy.

THE EYES of all look to You,
> *and You give them their food at the proper time.*
> *You open your hand*
> *and satisfy the desires of every living thing...*

ANOTHER BEND in the path brought them in view of the friary gates and his song suddenly evaporated. He stopped still and Ermentrude ran into him, butting his thigh with her head.

A procession of weary-looking men was trudging up the

road from Armonia. Fabrizio would usually have hurried forward to meet them, but there was something in their demeanor that made him instead step behind a scrub tree and watch as they approached the gates of San Stigliano. The goats showed no interest at all in the strangers, and took the opportunity to sprawl in the grass and rest.

There were six men, all dressed in short gray robes that exposed their bare feet. The robes hung limply. Some were torn, a few shamefully dirty. The strangers carried nothing with them, no pouch, no bags of provisions. Several used walking sticks, but these were only the slim, crooked branches of trees, such as one might find on the ground after a storm. They were wild-looking, and desperately poor, just as Old Leonard had said. With a rush of remembrance, Fabrizio realized who they were, and, with a sickening feeling, why they were here.

These were the Spirituals, Franciscan friars who led lives of extreme poverty to show the world that they had not given up what they considered the true way of St. Francis. They denounced Franciscans who lived in convents surrounded by walls and ceilings and books and regular meals. Even their shorter robes, closer to the style of a peasant, proclaimed their protest against Franciscans like Fabrizio, who wore longer robes and even shoes if a task required it. They carried no pouches because Judas had used a pouch. Seeing them, Fabrizio felt overly aware of the small burlap sack that hung off his rope belt, the one that carried his food on his days in the hills.

But these Spirituals were also rebels. In spite of the commands of the pope and all church authority, they had separated themselves from the others in the Order and claimed to be the truest of all Franciscans, following the poverty of Christ and the poverty of Saint Francis as no one else did.

According to a letter from Cardinal Scantoni, the overseer of this particular dispute, which the Guardian had read out loud to them after evening prayer several weeks ago, a meeting between a group of rigorist Franciscan friars—he had refused to call them Spirituals—and the pope's inquisitors was to be held this autumn. The Friary of San Stigliano was to be the place of meeting, and the cardinal had ordered a Dominican inquisitor to resolve this crisis.

So these friars at the gates must be the expected rigorists. Which meant that a group of Dominicans must be riding hard from the pope's palace in Avignon even now with one purpose. To persuade the Spirituals into obedience.

The men slowed their pace as they came near the heavy, wooden gates of the friary, standing open though they were. Fabrizio stiffened, peering through the leaves of the scrub tree. If the men were aware of his presence, or that of the goats, they did not show it.

Yet even still, he studied the men on the road with curiosity. How could a man choose to be so very, very poor? To deliberately choose not to know when he would be able to eat again? What would make him do such a thing? And how could someone be angry with those who did not choose to be so very poor? Fabrizio did not understand it.

Several long moments passed and the short-robed friars still hesitated on the road. They clumped together, heads turning and bobbing, some emphatic discussion going on amongst them. Fabrizio began to wonder at the delay.

Surely, the Spirituals had no fear of entering the gates.

There was nothing to fear in San Stigliano. It was the best and truest place to live in all the world. Whose heart could not lift just walking through the gates as his did every single day? No, it must be the Spirituals' abhorrence of such a community of friars. And a distaste for the very goods and buildings the community appeared to own and use.

The pealing of the tower bell interrupted their talk. Its noon summons to prayer could not be denied. The poor friars formed themselves into a group of little rows—two, by two, by two, as if they were soldiers preparing for battle—and entered the friary walls.

Fabrizio waited on the hillside until the last of them had disappeared into the courtyard. At the tenth peal of the bell, he ushered his goats the rest of the way down the slope and passed through the open gates, herding his charges toward their pen in the stables.

He, of course, would have nothing to do with the looming theological debates. Kerstan and their Guardian would attend to that. He was glad it was theirs to do and not his. He had learned to read and write fairly well and had qualified and earned the designation of priest, but he had a gift for goats and animals, like the humblest of lay brothers. Or, as their Guardian had told him once, "a gift like Saint Francis himself."

He would do his work, say his prayers, tend the goats, avoid the Spirituals, and live, as he did every day, this good Franciscan life that was God's gift to him.

2

———

Fabrizio was late to noon prayer, but such it was with their friary. A community of active friars, always moving through the town amongst the people, tending to ills or to such chores as could not easily be stopped, had the habit of saying their prayers and chanting their psalms as they went. It distinguished the friars from the cloistered monks people often assumed they were.

Fabrizio prayed aloud as he saw the goats safely back to their home in the small stable, gave them fresh water, and laid windfall apples in their manger. Though he worked quickly, he did not enter the chapel until the beginning of the last psalm.

The brothers that could leave their duties for noon prayer had taken seats on the left side of the chapel. The Spirituals fit easily onto one bench on the right side. People from the town had scattered themselves in the benches behind as usual. Light poured in from the high windows and reflected off the walls, white-washed for just that purpose.

The only color in the chapel came from the tapestry that hung on the wall behind the altar. Rich with golds and reds and greens, it depicted the heavenly city, the great throne of God above it, and the river of life flowing beneath. A master hand had woven in the words: *Whoever is thirsty, let him come. Whoever wishes, let him take the free gift of the water of life.* Donatello's father had given the tapestry to the friary in celebration of Donatello's twenty-first birthday. Fabrizio loved the sight of it. What would the Spirituals think of it, he wondered.

He stepped quietly down the side aisle to his seat. His brothers seemed to be chanting the psalms louder than usual, as if volume were a defense against potential heresy. Emilian raised an eyebrow as Fabrizio slid onto the bench next to him, but did not waver in his energetic singing.

During the series of amens that followed the psalm, Fabrizio stole a glance at the Spirituals. They had lowered their hoods and uncovered their heads for worship. Two had gray hair, the rest brown or black. It was hard to tell from where he sat. None of them, at least, had horns growing out of their heads.

He whispered this in a light-hearted tone to Emilian, who shook his head from side to side. "None *visible*," he whispered back.

The Guardian stood up and raised his hand to speak the blessing over those gathered.

THE LORD BLESS you and keep you.
    The Lord make His face shine upon you.
    The Lord turn His face toward you and give you peace.

THIS WAS a part of worship that Fabrizio treasured. He held very still, savoring the sound of every word. Hadn't the Lord told Moses and Aaron to say these words over His people? And then promised to bless every time? Even in this stark, white-washed chapel with its broken ceiling, Fabrizio could feel God's blessing falling on them.

As the final amen was spoken, the townspeople got to their feet and left the chapel. The Guardian motioned to the friars who remained, inviting them all to sit down again.

Fabrizio stole another glance at the Spirituals. What had they thought of the Guardian's blessing, coming as it did from the mouth of one whom they considered an enemy? The row of faces was solemn and resolute. The one on the end, the only one he could see in full, seemed tense, as if under a very great pressure.

"Today," the Guardian began, "we welcome these Franciscans who travel the country with their leader Venedictos." He indicated the gray-haired man on the aisle. "We hope your time with us will be beneficial to all."

The words were gracious and graciously spoken. Venedictos merely inclined his head, acknowledging that he had heard.

The Guardian smiled and nodded anyway. "Brother Benefice will show you to the rooms we have prepared for you in our humble dormitory above the kitchen. That is," he looked at them inquiringly, "if that is acceptable to you?"

Venedictos got to his feet. "Our Lord Christ had nowhere to lay His head," he said sternly. Pointedly.

"But surely," replied the Guardian, in gentle tones, "when

our Lord stayed at Peter's home in order to heal his mother-in-law, He accepted a pillow and bed?"

Placid, calm-looking Benefice had risen and stood waiting at the Guardian's side. Benefice was a wise choice. He had a childlike simplicity and a countenance as tranquil as a cabbage—something Cantor, who dearly loved to match wits, had often complained about.

After some moments, Venedictos nodded, and the Spirituals rose and followed Benefice out of the chapel.

The friars of San Stigliano remained seated. Only after the door closed behind the last of the Spirituals, did the Guardian open his mouth again.

"My dear brothers, we have all just seen the challenge that has come to us today. We have heard of its coming, and now it is upon us.

"But I do not refer to the poorest friars who were sitting on this bench. I am thinking of the challenge that will come to each one of us in our hearts."

Fabrizio felt uncomfortable at this and shifted on his bench. Emilian, he noted, held very still, his attention centered on the Guardian. Fabrizio tried to follow his example.

"You know we work hard to be good Franciscans, to be good Christians in that way. We have made our vows of poverty, and we will be faithful to them.

"What has been loaned to us for our use, we use for God's glory—the books, the library, the gardens. Not one of us has a group of personal items that we claim to the exclusion of others.

"As you all know, the friary itself was a gift from a dying

man to the church. Not to us, to the church. And we use it as the church allows us to. We look to no rich benefactor for favors, no matter how often Donatello begs me to let him finish the work on the chapel roof."

There was laughter at this and Fabrizio couldn't help smiling too. Each one of them had heard Donatello's insistence and the Guardian's equally insistent refusals.

"I do not need to tell you," the Guardian continued, "that these Spirituals do not see things that way. This is where the challenge comes to all of us. Some of them may be looking for offense, looking for where we have done wrong. They may even go so far as to accuse us of being false to our vows of poverty, hinting of mortal sin."

Emilian's face hardened at this. Fabrizio felt his stomach tighten. He gave a quick glance at the others, but could not tell what they were thinking beyond the serious looks on their faces.

"Handle yourselves wisely," the Guardian urged. "Go gently among them. If they wish to speak with you, speak to them. But do not be pulled into an argument. Be gentle in your words and in your manner. Leave room for the Lord Himself to speak to hearts. It is better that they hear His voice, than have earfuls of ours."

When they had been dismissed, Fabrizio walked slowly out of the chapel doors and stopped in the open square. His gaze was drawn to the upper windows of the dormitory where guests of the friary usually stayed. Were they housing invaders? Malicious ones like scorpions ready to sting with poison? He tried to shake off the disturbing feeling and turned to join Emilian and Kerstan who stood nearby.

"And so the questioning is to begin soon, Kerstan?" Emilian said, in a low voice.

"As soon as the inquisitor arrives," Kerstan replied.

"I do not envy you your listening and recording of their debates," said Emilian. "That Venedictos is ready for a fight."

Kerstan sighed. "It must be done. Our Guardian cannot always attend, and I am to be his eyes and ears, listening for him and for the *Custode*. This will be an important event in the life of the friary, and it must be noted with all care."

Fabrizio felt a rush of admiration for Kerstan and his great gift for words and learning. In Fabrizio's hard and lonely childhood, for one scant year he had had a friend. And that friend too had loved words and learning.

"Does this mean the copying of the book of Romans must wait?" Fabrizio asked.

Emilian frowned. "How can it? The scriveners are already here. And one of the copies is for a future Visconti bride."

"It will not need to wait." Kerstan spoke the words as firmly as if he were swearing an oath. "Even inquisitors have to eat and drink and rest, and when they do, I will hurry to the library and direct the work there. We will be faithful to our commission—a commission that earns us no money. I must draw attention to that fact, in the presence of the Spirituals. The Visconti money pays the scribes, buys ingredients for the ink, and purchases the expensive parchment and leather for the covers. And that is all. You must tell them that if they ask."

Kerstan sighed again. "Well, I am off to the library now. Where are you going, my friends?"

"I have a class to teach in town," said Emilian. "And you, Fabrizio?"

Fabrizio couldn't keep his mind off those stern, judgmental Spiritual friars. If they were in the dormitory, he would not go in there. The sweeping of the halls could wait. "I think I will help Gustave for the rest of the day. We have so many to feed now."

They nodded and turned to go on their ways while he walked to the far side of the building and poked his head into the kitchen door. Gustave was there as always, aproned and sweating in the heat of cooking fires, stirring something in the large black cauldron. Several of the kitchen boys looked on.

Gustave welcomed Fabrizio's help without question. "Just make sure you wash up to your elbows. I do not want my soup and loaves to smell like your goats."

Fabrizio laughed as he splashed water on his arms —laughed because he knew Gustave meant for him to—and answered as he always did. "Ah, Gustave, you know that the female goats do not smell."

HE WORKED in the kitchen with Gustave the rest of the day, leaving only to take the goats out for a short afternoon's forage. They ate and frolicked in a grassy scrubland just north of the friary. The day remained gently warm with just the breath of a wind. From somewhere farther down in the valley, smoke and the smell of burning stubble lifted to his nostrils. Perhaps Antonio had persuaded another farmer to prepare his fields this way for autumn planting.

Fabrizio returned the goats to their stable, and took himself to the chapel on time for afternoon prayer. Surprisingly, the Spirituals did not appear. Afterwards, the San Stigliano friars lingered inside the chapel door.

"Their wandering life may have kept them from being attuned to the canonical hours," said Kerstan.

Emilian scowled. "Any half-wit can recognize the sound of a church bell and guess what it means."

Fabrizio meant to keep silent, but the image of haggard, thin faces came to mind. He found himself saying, "Perhaps they are tired and unwell."

"They are," said Emilian. "Thoroughly unwell. Unwell in body, mind, and spirit!"

Benefice was unperturbed. "They are probably in prayer where they are right now, just as we so often are."

"And praying that they may be kept pure from our evil earthliness," put in Cantor.

Fabrizio walked back to the kitchen thinking of what his brother friars had said and wishing that this controversy could be removed from San Stigliano. He shook the wishes from his mind. Hadn't he given up such wishing with childhood?

He thought of the urgent discussion he had seen outside the gates. The Spirituals had not wanted to enter for whatever reason. What coercion had this Cardinal Scantoni used to make them come?

Well, this was not his business anyway. These matters were for the learned who pored over books and examined meanings as part of their daily lives. They would be the ones to talk and argue and debate. And he, the goatherd, would stay out of everyone's way. But he would pray and pray that all would soon be over, leaving San Stigliano unscathed, leaving their lives here untouched.

He had been sent by Gustave to the garden to pull carrots for the evening meal. Just before he entered the garden gate, the sound of some commotion on the road made him stop. In a few moments, two splendid-looking coaches drove through the friary gates and into the square, reining in their horses in a cloud of late summer dust.

Several men on horseback escorted them. These dismounted quickly and hurried to open the coach doors. Robed men emerged, dressed in Dominican black.

As they stepped to the ground, Fabrizio saw the toes of leather boots appear from underneath their robes. Strong boots with wooden soles. The kind that could crush a man with no shoes on.

One of the men raised his head to look around him, calling out, "Guardian Amadeus Walerian!"

It was a deep voice, a commanding voice. The Dominican that had called out paused and looked around the square, as if expecting to see their Guardian come scurrying out from some small door in response. Instead, Kerstan hastened from the library doors, bowing and motioning toward the library invitingly. He gave instructions to the drivers, pointing them to the stables. The rest of the men followed him up the steps and through the heavy oaken doors which led to the Guardian's study.

Fabrizio filled his basket with all the carrots ready for eating and returned to the kitchen. "There will be more for dinner, Gustave," he told the cook. "At least seven more."

Gustave looked up from the spit where he was tying a row

of chickens, a gift from the mayor of their town. "The inquisitors have come?" he asked quietly.

Cantor entered the back door just in time to hear this. "Yes, they have come," he said, "and are as fierce-looking as any Dominicans I've ever seen. They look used to better food and twice as much of it as we Franciscans."

Gustave frowned. "There will be plenty as usual," he said. "And chicken to add to the soup for the others tonight."

Cantor sighed. "Chicken. The smell of it will make me wish I were ill, just so I could have some."

The kitchen door swung open again and the tall form of Donatello, their procurator, entered. With his red surcoat and dark blue mantle, he stood out boldly as he always did when surrounded with clouds of Franciscan gray.

"Gustave, the Guardian would like me to tell you that there will be at least ten more at dinner."

"Ten?" Gustave waved his arm in Fabrizio's direction. "They said seven!"

"Their servants will be here soon. They stopped in town to make some purchases. I don't know how long they will be at the friary, but your resources will be strained even more. Gustave, make sure you tell me what you need before your supplies get too low. I will keep a close eye on the money I have in account." Donatello shook his head. "Where is Benefice? Are there rooms enough?" He did not wait for an answer, but left in haste, his blue robes swirling around him.

Gustave took a few steps toward Fabrizio. "Why Dominicans?" he asked in a low voice. "Why not Franciscan authorities?"

"I don't know," Fabrizio answered. "Kerstan says the pope likes Dominicans."

Cantor glanced up at the smoke-stained plastered ceiling. The floor above housed the sleeping rooms. "Do you think the Dominicans would like to share rooms in the dormitory with their friends the Spirituals?" His tone was purposefully innocent. He grinned at Fabrizio. "Think of all the lovely arguments they could have."

"Shush and go," said Gustave, "or I'll put you to work. The kitchen boys don't need to hear your chatter."

"Quintus sent me for mustard for the infirmary," said Cantor.

"Take it then," said Gustave, "and don't be greedy with it. Fabrizio, I need those carrots chopped." He leaned closer and whispered. "I don't want the boys to use my knife yet. Especially Leo. He could lose one of his fingers."

The kitchen slowly filled with the enchanting aromas of chicken and onion and carrot and bean. Soup bubbled in the large black pots over the fire while Leo stirred them each in turn, only burning himself once. After pulling apart the roasted chickens, Gustave added them to the company pot with pepper and ginger. He swirled the spices into the Franciscan pot too.

Ginger was an expensive spice, and could be seen by some as an unwonted luxury. Yet it came regularly to their community as a gift from Donatello's father. It was one of the few gifts from their wealthy procurator that the Guardian allowed. The ginger flavored the soup and healed the friars' stomachs at the same time.

"Would you rather fill the bowls or serve them?" Gustave asked, waving a ladle at Fabrizio.

"Fill them." He took the ladle, reached for the first

wooden bowl waiting on the table close by, and scooped a large serving of the hearty soup into it.

"How many bowls for company?" he asked the older boy who held the tray ready to receive them. "Have any of the poor from town come?"

"Four and two small children," the boy answered promptly. "Six scribes are staying tonight. And the inquisitor's group makes ten more. So, twenty-two bowls for now."

"So, are you going to be a mathematician, then?" asked Fabrizio, filling more bowls while he talked. "You are quick with your numbers."

"Donatello thinks I have an aptitude for accounting work," the boy answered proudly. "I have loved numbers all my life."

"Well then, how many bowls will your tray hold?"

"Eight. I need two more."

"Here's seven. Now eight. On your way."

A small, quiet boy held out his tray next. He said nothing, for his voice had been injured when he was very young and he had not spoken since. Benefice was teaching him to ring the bell.

Fabrizio smiled at him. "Was that you who rang the bell for Vespers this evening?"

The boy nodded his head a little shyly.

"I thought you did very well," said Fabrizio, setting a bowl on his tray. "It must be great fun to make such a very big noise."

The boy grinned from ear to ear.

It was good work ladling soup. It felt like filling souls. The sight of the full, bubbling kettles thrilled him. They were weapons in the war, powerful weapons meant to drive away the awful enemy of hunger.

Only a few Armonian *poverelli* had come up the hill to eat tonight. He wanted more and more to come. Let all the empty stomachs of the poor in Armonia come. Because tonight he, Fabrizio, was wielding this ladle against the darkness of poverty. And in the eyes of his imagination, he saw himself vanquishing it.

3

———

When Fabrizio poked his head through the kitchen door and into the dining hall, it was already filled with people. A large fireplace dominated one wall. Four long tables, each with one end toward the fireplace and their other ends toward the back of the room, provided most of the seating. One of the center tables, and especially the end closest to the fire, was reserved for the *poverelli* and Fabrizio was glad to see the people seated there.

The other center table was occupied by the Guardian and Donatello and rows of men from the Dominican party. The table on the far side held a group of launderers, and the scholars and scriveners who had decided not to spend their money in town tonight. Benefice was among them, probably matching his memory for proverbs against the best of the scholars. The table with its end closest to the kitchen door was where Fabrizio usually sat.

Along the back wall, at right angles to all the others, was a fifth table, seldom used because even in the best of weather a cool current of air always seemed to move across it. Fabrizio was annoyed to find that there, seated on either side, the Spiritual friars had stationed themselves. Vicious drafts already set the oil lamps flickering. The dancing light made the shadows on their faces even more harsh and disapproving, and the backs of those facing away from the room, more reproachful.

Fabrizio ate with Kerstan, Emilian, and Cantor. Prentice, one of Kerstan's scriveners, joined them. He had an air of confidence about him and deftly pulled the chicken from his soup with thin, ink-stained fingers. As he chewed vigorously, he talked. Oblivious to the discord in the room, his mind was filled instead with the elaborate ritual Kerstan had devised for the copiers.

"He has us all working together," said Prentice. "Imagine the reader, another man who stands beside him, and then me at my desk with my ink and quills with a watcher of my own. And not just me—every scribe has a watcher."

As Prentice continued, Fabrizio stole glances at the Dominicans just beyond, and the Spirituals at their table. What did they think of such a dining atmosphere? Many convents and friaries ate in contemplative silence. But here, friendly talk was encouraged, as long as it did not become boisterous. This was because the *poverelli* were always invited and the Guardian of San Stigliano wanted to welcome them to a cheerful place.

But what judgments would the others make? How quickly one could interpret things wrongly. Fabrizio felt uneasy and tried to turn his attention back to Prentice, who was waving a chicken bone at them while he talked.

"The reader reads the next sentence in its entirety. Then the watcher reads it again so I know what long and short words I have coming up. Placement is very important," he said, gesturing with the chicken bone. "Then the reader reads the first three words in the sentence, echoed by the watcher. I repeat those three words echoed by my watcher. The reader reads just the first word. We echo it. He spells it letter by letter, with echoes of course, and I write the word on the parchment."

"Tedious," said Cantor, staring at the chicken bone while Prentice drew a breath.

"It *is* tedious," said Prentice. "And unlike any work I have ever done. Usually I sit at a table and write directly from the copy myself."

"But this is necessary," said Kerstan, firmly. "We are copying from an error-less exemplar and making a number of copies at once. It is my job to make sure no errors are introduced. How could we do less for the Visconti, for Matteo the Lord of Milan? Or, for the Lord of Heaven himself?"

"How do you not lose your place when you are doing the reading?" Fabrizio asked Kerstan. "I often do."

Kerstan held up his bare hands. "Linen gloves. No one can touch the original without them. Wearing them, I move the lead weights on the exemplar word by word and line by line. The watcher makes sure that my finger does not slip." He looked at Prentice. "The whole process goes more smoothly than it sounds."

Fabrizio could not comprehend how a person could even think of such a plan. His admiration for Kerstan grew.

Prentice tore another piece of chicken from the bone and flicked it into his mouth. "I will have the entire book of

Romans memorized by the time I am finished, because of how often its words will be said to me and how often I will have to say them back."

"You probably will," said Fabrizio. "That would be wonderful. Kerstan is a natural tutor. Only with his constant help did I become a priest."

"I am a scribe, not a priest," replied Prentice, a little sharply.

"Where did you finish today?" asked Cantor.

"Today we prepared the parchment, measuring out each line." Prentice spoke with annoyance. "The ink was not ready until the afternoon, so we practiced Kerstan's method over and over before we finally began."

"And the last phrase of today was…?" Cantor asked again.

"The last phrase I copied today was, '*and you also are among those who are called to belong to Jesus Christ.*'"

Emilian leaned into the conversation. "That would still be early in chapter one?"

Kerstan nodded over his soup bowl. "But we have begun and that is the great thing. Prentice is one of the best copiers I have ever seen. I'm sure the finished book will be a thing of beauty and the Visconti family will be pleased. And if they are pleased, there could be more requests coming."

Prentice's attitude mellowed with Kerstan's praise. He joined the conversation again, a more genial light on his face. "What I don't understand is how a small friary like yours can have an expensive Bible. I've worked in large monasteries that have only the Gospel of Mark, or the letter to the Galatians."

"I can answer that," said Cantor. "Donatello's father. He gave it as a gift to the friary in honor of Donatello's sixteenth birthday, about, what, eight years ago? If we were monks and not friars, we could sell Fabrizio's cheese and purchase many more books."

Emilian frowned at him. "We are friars for good reason, Cantor. We don't need the profits from selling cheese." His voice was hushed and guarded. "And we have books enough on the library shelves."

Fabrizio stole another glance at the Spirituals' table. Could they have heard? Would they take Cantor's usual teasing for a serious matter that must be addressed?

Cantor looked amused. "I am a friar because I have made a vow to be a friar. To be a *poor* friar. I do not regret it. Even if I did not get chicken in my bowl."

"This is not helpful, Cantor," said Kerstan, looking quickly at where the Spirituals sat.

"We were speaking of cheese," said Prentice, a hungry look in his eye. "Yours?" he looked at Fabrizio.

Fabrizio shook his head. "It's not my cheese. Gustave makes it from his mother's recipe. I only milk the goats." But he got to his feet, glad to remove himself from fears of what the Spirituals might be thinking. He picked up the empty bowls to take with him. "I think it's time to serve it now anyway."

Gustave had already cut up the great soft cheese round, arranging the creamy white chunks on the oak cheese board in neat piles. Leo stood ready with the refilled bread bowl. Fabrizio picked up the board and returned to the dining hall, Leo close behind him.

He went first to the small group of *poverelli* at the table by the fireplace. Two old men sat there; one was missing an arm. Next to them, a young woman with two thin children. An old woman sat a little ways away from the others, lifting soup in a shaking spoon slowly to her mouth.

"Eat, my friends, and welcome," Fabrizio said as he placed cheese and bread on the table.

He spoke a blessing over each one of them, then turned to the rest of the tables and hesitated, feeling the tension in the room. The Guardian caught his eye and beckoned him to where he sat at the Dominican table. Donatello, at his side, looked more regal than usual, a swath of gold edging his blue mantle.

The black-robed visitors did not seem as fierce as they had before. Seated at their meal, they looked like any men would after many days of travel. Their soup bowls were already empty and they appeared eager to try the cheese.

The Guardian said their names to Fabrizio as he held out the cheese board to them, but afterwards he could only remember three of the names. Nobilus, the leader of the group, had a thick black beard. Yet the skin of his face was pale and white, as one who had been away from the sun for a long time. When he spoke his thanks, Fabrizio recognized the voice who had called out the Guardian's name in the courtyard that afternoon.

Manus wore the clothes of a judge or an official, not of a religious order. His robes were well-made, of good weave, but were not as expensively-fashioned as Donatello's. His lips barely moved under his mustache as he said his thanks, but his eyes studied Fabrizio. He had the eyes of a shopowner who did not trust the small boy who had just stepped inside.

Titus, the next Dominican, had a smile both on his lips and in his eyes. His red-brown beard was cut close to his chin;

his amber eyes filled with benevolence. "Thank you, Brother Fabrizio," he said.

"You are very welcome," Fabrizio answered.

The Dominican group cleared the cheese board completely. As the last was taken, Nobilus spoke to the Guardian.

"Well then, Walerian," he said. "Now that we have had the pleasure of experiencing your dining hall, and meeting your friars, I am more than ready to share the real dinner with you in your private rooms."

Even his smile had command in it.

"I am afraid I do not understand you, Brother Nobilus," the Guardian answered gently. "This is the real dinner. There is no food waiting in my private rooms, as you say. And I can assure you that no food will ever be waiting there. I will share in the humility of eating such food as you see with my friars. We have nothing else."

Nobilus opened his mouth, as if to speak, then closed it firmly, while the Guardian waited, a kind look on his face. Nobilus shook his head then opened his mouth again.

"I have only referred to the habit other convents have of receiving their guests. And before you hasten to disagree with me, I do mean *Franciscan* convents."

"I will not disagree with you. For aren't such convents the reason that the poorest of our brethren have felt the need to protest so firmly? Sharing in the poverty of Christ is surely at the heart of the Franciscan way of life."

Nobilus lifted his chin with apparent scorn. "You Franciscans! You give importance to things that should not be—"

Donatello broke in. "Would you and your guests care to visit my home in town this evening, Brother Nobilus? I would be happy to entertain you with another supper so you may rest from your travels."

Fabrizio could linger by the table no longer. The tone of the disagreement disturbed him. He returned to the kitchen and refilled the cheese board. But he hesitated in the doorway, wondering where it would be proper to serve next. Never had the dining room of his home seemed such a awkward place.

He purposely ignored Cantor's impatient wave as he surveyed the room. Perhaps he should go to the other side of the fireplace to Benefice and the launderers and scribes. From here, he could pick out Benefice's eager voice among the others.

"*Arbor naturam dat fructibus...*" Sure enough. Benefice was entertaining his table with the catalog of proverbs he carried in his mind.

A silent draft sent the oil lamps flickering again and drew his attention to the back table where the Spirituals sat. Some were eating slowly; some soberly studied the room. The light illuminated one face particularly, a young face, without health or energy. This youngest of the group had a pinched, worn, even haunted look—the kind of look that came from long acquaintance with hunger.

Fabrizio could not stand to see such a look on such a face. A sharp pain stabbed at his own stomach, as if the youth's hunger had become his. He walked past Cantor's upraised hand and the subtle protests from his friends and carried the board to the cold wall holding it out to the young man. Too late, Fabrizio realized he should have offered it to Venedictos first. But it was too late. He stayed where he was.

"Please, take some," he said, trying to smile. "Take all that you need. There is more in the kitchen."

He was aware that the room had quieted somewhat, and that more eyes than he wished were watching him bring cheese to the obstinate Spirituals. *Well, what of it,* he argued inside his mind. *They are here. And I will feed them.*

He moved among them, watching as they reached silently, and to all appearances gratefully, for Gustave's homemade cheese. A gray-bearded, wrinkled face with a short hooked nose took its first bite and smiled. Fabrizio felt gratified.

He came to the end of the little band, the last two friars. The one across the table took his portion, nodding thanks, but the one nearest, whose back had been to the room suddenly grabbed Fabrizio's arm.

"Fabrizio?" The voice was full of disbelief. "Is it really you, Fabrizio? Here?"

Startled, Fabrizio looked into a pair of lively brown eyes. Beyond all reason he knew them! And beneath them was a hint of the smile that had once been more familiar than his own.

Fabrizio felt dizzy. His stomach clenched and his heart began to pound. He glanced around the room. The eyes of the Dominicans were on him. Manus was staring outright. From his own table, Cantor too was watching, a curious expression on his face.

Fabrizio shook his head violently and pulled away. "No. No."

Leo, who had been following Fabrizio with the bread bowl, stepped back also, suddenly unsure.

The poor friar's expression clouded, and his hand fell from Fabrizio's arm. "Forgive me," he said, turning back toward his fellows. Fabrizio still awkwardly held out the board for a few moments, but the friar made no attempt to take some cheese.

He took the board back to the kitchen, half full though it still was. Without deferring to Gustave, he motioned to the older kitchen boy, calling him from the washbasin.

"Finish serving the cheese. The far right table and the far left. The middle and back have already been served." The boy nodded and moved briskly to take the board.

Not all of them were served, protested a voice in his mind. *One of the poor ones did not get cheese. Why did I pull away? Why did I leave?*

He ignored the voice and darted past Gustave's puzzled face, through the back door of the kitchen, and out into the cool night air.

4

____

Out in the courtyard, Fabrizio pressed his hands against the sides of his head, trying to ease the pressure so he could think. The last glow of the late summer day was still in the sky, but a shadow-laced twilight ruled the friary square.

He paced the packed earth of the courtyard, going around the large oak in its center, ducking at the last minute to avoid one of its long arm-like branches in the dusk, then back to the kitchen door. Out and around, again and again. His mind moved as furiously as his feet.

Sereno? Sereno was among the enemies of the Franciscan community? How could that be? *Lord God in heaven, how could that be?* It was like finding the sun in a pile of refuse. Or a star from the sky sloshing in the waste pit! Sereno's face had changed, grown from boyhood to adult, but the eyes, the smile, and the impulsive manner had been so like him. What did this mean?

A crash sounded from the kitchen. Leo had probably

dropped a pottery dish. Gustave complained that Leo broke at least one each week and that soon they would have none left.

Fabrizio turned to go back inside. He must not draw attention or questioning to himself. Must not do anything that would separate him from these convent friars who were the brothers of his life. After all, he was an obedient Franciscan, not a troublesome rigorist.

But what had happened to Sereno?

He pushed open the door and was surprised to find the kitchen full of people. All the servers and almost all the friars were there. Gustave was scolding a red-faced Leo in the corner. Benefice scraped out one of the large kettles at the broad sink, while Emilian talked intently to Kerstan over the worktable. Donatello sat on a stool listening to them, looking like a colorful bluebird in a nest of Franciscan gray.

Cantor was taking the bowls the silent server was handing him, and replacing them on their shelves. When he saw Fabrizio, the curious look returned to his face. Fabrizio bent his head to avoid it and immediately set to work picking up the pieces of the large mixing bowl.

"Fabrizio, what did that Spiritual—" Cantor began.

Donatello chose that moment to speak over the commotion. "Now that Fabrizio is back, I wanted to tell all of you that I purchased the wood for the chapel roof trusses today."

"Ah, wonderful!" cried Emilian.

Kerstan stood up and began to clap quietly.

Donatello went on. "But I must remind everyone again to be careful with everything. There must be no waste. The account is lower than I would like it to be now."

The words must have been hard for Leo to hear after breaking the bowl.

"I like being a Franciscan," said Cantor lightly, "and not having to even think about money."

Gustave patted Leo on the back, and joined the rest of them. "I do not waste, Donatello," he said, "and you know that well. But with seventeen or eighteen more stomachs to feed, you must make allowances for that in your numbers."

Benefice poured the last of the dirty water from the iron pot and moved to rehang it over the fire. "All the additional mouths will not be here long," he said mildly. "'*Subtrahe ligna focis, flammam restinguere si vis.* If you would quench the fire, take off the fuel.' The false ones will be debated into agreement. The Head Inquisitor will make them see their error. Then they will repent and go on their way. All will be well." He smiled and rubbed his hands together as he looked around at all of them.

Fabrizio stopped sweeping to stare at him, suddenly hopeful.

Emilian shook his head slowly. "Do you think it will be as easy as that, Kerstan?"

Kerstan frowned. "Those calling themselves Spirituals have been imprisoned in France and in the Marches of Ancona. I've heard rumors of tortures used on them. I wish Benefice were right. But we really don't know. I hope we will be spared the grimness of such things. The Spirituals can be violent too. Some of them took over several convents near Siena. They threw out the friars who lived there and refused to give the convent back to them."

"That's—that's war!" said Emilian.

Fabrizio held his broom tightly. A horrible image filled

his mind, of being put outside the walls of San Stigliano and never being allowed to return. Could Venedictos and his band do this? He cleared the lump from his throat. "What will it take? To—to make things right?"

"I think it will take much patience and many, many words," Kerstan replied. "And even then, words may not have the power to turn the rebels."

"But they don't consider themselves rebels," said Emilian irritably. "To them *we* are the rebels. *We* are the false ones."

"Ah yes," said Cantor wryly, "and how many words would it take to turn us from our ways?"

"Be quiet, Cantor," said Emilian. "We have no need to turn from our ways! The question is how long will they do this? How long will they insist that their poverty is more Franciscan than our poverty?"

"Hush!" said Kerstan. "You are too loud. Do you want the Dominicans in here?"

Donatello got to his feet, caught up the folds of his dark blue mantle, and stylishly draped them over one arm. "You remind me. I am giving the Dominicans a late supper in my home tonight. I must be going." He pushed open the door to the dining room, letting it fall shut behind him.

Fabrizio dumped the broken shards of pottery into the waste bucket. He felt miserable with all this talk. If such a learned man as Kerstan held out little chance for peace, what was going to happen to San Stigliano?

Kerstan rubbed his clean-shaven chin. "I don't think they will ever stop, Emilian," he said quietly. "The Spirituals, I mean. There will always be disagreements about the poverty needed to best emulate Christ, the apostles, and Saint Francis."

"Then why have they come?" cried Emilian, ignoring Kerstan's move to shush him again. "Why are they here?"

"How could you refuse if Cardinal Scantoni asked you?" said Cantor.

Before Emilian could respond to this, Kerstan spoke. "They are here because we have a Bible that both the Spirituals and the Dominicans can turn to in their debate. And also copies of all the papal bulls concerning the Franciscans."

Cantor's voice held a note of mockery that only left him during prayers or in the sickroom. "All this, of course, is to cover the real reason San Stigliano was chosen. A lot of noise can be made in these hills and no one in the greater world need ever hear of it. San Stigliano would make a better monastery than friary, secluded as it is. The debates can rage as loud as they wish and go on for all eternity, and the rest of Europe would never know."

"'Far from court, far from care,'" quoted Benefice.

"You're forgetting about the mail that travels to Avignon every week, Cantor," said Emilian. "And Rome, and Florence, and Genoa, and Milan."

Cantor shrugged his shoulders. "News is news only if people read it."

"Don't fool yourself, Cantor," said Kerstan, shaking his head. "The papacy, the cardinals, the kings of Europe, and the whole Franciscan chapter are paying very close attention to what is happening in our friary."

Fabrizio felt sick. This whole affair was more serious, more dangerous, than he had first thought. A wave of sadness filled him and he felt himself floating on its tide. He was startled when Cantor spoke abruptly to him.

"One of the poor ones seemed to know you."

Fabrizio's stomach lurched, but he shook his head calmly, pretending to have no concern. "No, they were just grateful for the cheese."

"More grateful than the Dominicans, it seems," said Gustave shortly, as he watched Leo carefully set out the large wooden bowls for tomorrow's bread-making.

Fabrizio imitated Cantor's shrug in reply. He turned from his brothers and placed the broom in the corner bin Gustave had made for it.

"But Fabrizio, you at least talked with the poor friars," said Emilian, What did you think of them?"

Fabrizio swallowed carefully. "I think they were hungry men eating their dinner," he said slowly.

"That is all?" said Cantor, raising one eyebrow.

"Look," said Fabrizio, more intensely than he meant to, "I am not a theologian, so I really have nothing to do with all this. I memorized the one hundred verses of Scripture our Guardian bade me when I joined the order. I say them every day without fail. Yet you all know that I was almost refused the honor of being a priest. A man's gifts can only go as far as they have been given." He glanced quickly at their faces, surprised at the defensiveness he felt. These were his brothers. He had no war with them.

"Let the inquisitors and theologians solve this," he continued, more gently. "They are the gifted ones. Men like our Guardian, and Kerstan, who with half a dozen scriveners is currently examining the book of Romans one careful word at a time."

He turned toward the outer door and held up his hand with the flourish of an actor. "As for me, I must go lead my goats in their Compline prayer." A few chuckles followed him into the cool night.

But Fabrizio was not laughing as he sat, miserable, on the stool in the middle of the goat pen, while his sleepy charges chose their places in the straw around him. He had received the shock of his life when Sereno grabbed his arm, and as a result, he had just lied to all his brothers. The only brothers he had ever had.

Ermentrude rubbed her head against his knee. He stroked her neck, combing her fine, long hair with his fingers. "Oh, Ermentrude, my friend, my friend. What am I to do?"

No comfort came to him. Instead, he saw Sereno's face in his mind's eye. Not with the bright look he wore when he had recognized Fabrizio, but with the dullness that filled his eyes as Fabrizio turned from recognizing him.

The bell for Compline rang out into the night. Fabrizio slid to his knees in the dirt and straw, and in confusion and shame bowed his head.

God, come to my assistance. Lord, make haste to help me…

5

——————

In the middle of the morning on the following day, Fabrizio made his way through the upper floor of San Stigliano's library. He had a half hour free before he was due for prayers and there was something he needed to see for himself.

Studious men, scholars, and scribes bent over their books, sharing the few tables. Some scriveners sharpened their quills for the next work session. Others stirred the gall nuts as they boiled over the library fire to make their ink. A smell like bitter figs penetrated the room.

At the far end of the library stood a chestnut door, a rectangle of brown in a stark, white wall. Fabrizio lifted the latch and quietly stepped through the doorway. He was in a long gallery room, a loft of sorts, from which one looked through a diamond-shaped wood lattice into the large council room below.

In this narrow loft, Kerstan sat at a table, working away with his wrapped pencil. Filled sheets of paper on the table next to him testified to his industry. Another stack of clean sheets waited their turn. Kerstan would spend his evenings copying the pencil writings onto real parchment with ink for a more permanent record. At the far end of the gallery stood the Guardian, soberly attentive to the voices that rose up from the room below.

Fabrizio bowed to them, then lowered himself into a seat and looked down into the large, square, white-washed room. It was sparely furnished, rarely in use except for special meetings. Built by the noble family, it had once been a room for dancing and merry-making. Today's proceedings were far more serious.

Long tables lined the side walls, each table with benches tucked between it and the wall behind, so those seated could write or lean on the table while facing the others in the room. At the table to the right, sat the row of Spiritual friars. Their hoods were thrown back, their arms folded, their expressions set as in stone.

The Dominican side, on the left, was a sea of movement. Black-robed figures shuffled through papers, paged through books from the piles on their table, wrinkled their foreheads while poring over them, and stabbed passages with their fingers, nodding knowingly. Whatever point their side had just made, they appeared satisfied with the support for it.

Nobilus stood at the side of his table, his dark beard contrasting with his pale face, just as his black robe contrasted with the white walls surrounding him. He made a magnificent figure, tall with strong shoulders, and a manner as commanding as any lord.

As Fabrizio watched, Venedictos got to his feet, preparing to speak. The Spiritual leader was as tall as

Nobilus, yet bony and gray and still somewhat stained. Seated next to his vacated spot was Sereno, or the one Fabrizio thought could be Sereno. For this was why he had come.

Upon waking this morning, a surge of hopeful feeling had told Fabrizio that he had been mistaken at dinner the night before. For all he knew, the friar who had grabbed his arm could have been anyone. Many men were impulsive. Many eyes familiar to him now.

Was this man the son of a shopkeeper Fabrizio used to sweep for? A priest's brother who had given him charity? As Fabrizio finished the goats' morning milking, he had counseled himself. It would be wise not to believe in a mere assumption. And it would be best if this man were not Sereno. Therefore, he must be someone else. Fabrizio peered through the screen at the activity in the room below.

"The main point is this." Venedictos' thin voice echoed off the bare walls. "Who is the higher authority?" he said, raising a bony finger in the air. "Christ or the Church? Christ the Head or the Church beneath Him? Why may we not honor our Lord by living as He did? As Saint Francis himself did? As all Franciscans are supposed to?"

He spread out his arms and looked around him as he spoke the last phrase, and his meaning was clear. San Stigliano's friars did not live the way Franciscans were supposed to live. Fabrizio felt his face grow warm.

"The Franciscan Order has fallen away from the very reason it was called into being. This friary itself is such an example! They do not follow Lady Poverty here."

Fabrizio glanced at the Guardian and Kerstan. How did they respond to such an accusation? The Guardian still watched in the same steady way. Kerstan shook his head grimly as he wrote down what Venedictos said.

"Christ's authority resides in His Church." Nobilus was the bass to the Spiritual leader's reedy tenor. He pronounced each word distinctly. Each had the sound of a muffled thunder blast. "You must acknowledge that," he said, emphasizing his statement with a thump of his fist on the table. "Saint Francis himself promised that whosoever shall be the head of this order shall be obedient to the pope and hold him in reverence."

Kerstan nodded in agreement as he quickly wrote the words.

On the Dominican side of the room, the men seated at the tables also wrote swiftly. None of the Spirituals were writing. Their table was empty. Perhaps they had not been given any paper. Fabrizio wondered if they had declined the use of it.

Even as he thought this, another black-robed figure stood up on the Dominican side, the one with the reddish hair and beard. Titus. He had rag paper and a wrapped pencil in his hand. He crossed the room quietly, careful to stay away from the debaters and held out the paper and pencil to the impulsive friar. The friar nodded and took them. Titus returned to his place.

As Fabrizio watched, the friar spread the paper flat with a swift motion of his left hand, first one corner, than the other, before putting his pencil to it with his right hand. It was a curious motion, one that he had seen no one else do. No one but Sereno. And he had seen him do it first as a boy, laying out his paper on a small wooden writing board in the garden behind his family's home.

Why do I do this, Fabrizio? Ah! It is good you ask. I do it because words are great things and I must make the paper ready for them.

Fabrizio dropped his gaze and rubbed his face in his hands. The worst was true. He could hope and wish it away no longer. Sereno belonged to this group of rebellious Spiritual friars.

A surge of anger filled him. Sereno, schooled to be at the side of any king or duke in the land, instead sat obediently at the side of a man who led him from town to town as a vagrant. What awful thing must have happened to bring this about?

Nobilus' voice carried even louder. "And it is the authority of the Church that determines the nature of the orders of monks and friars. An authority Saint Francis recognized."

Venedictos' attempted reply was stopped by a wave of the inquisitor's hand.

"We will not be addressing every topic you have in mind, Venedictos. And I am sure you have many. I have come from Avignon for one purpose, to hear your reply to my questions, and that is all. I have only two questions, but I must have the answer from each one of you."

Venedictos gave a sudden look of concern to the row of Spirituals, but he did not interrupt Nobilus. The inquisitor stepped to the center of the room and glared up and down the row of Spiritual faces.

"Only two questions," he repeated.

Sereno had stopped writing, his eyes on Nobilus.

The Dominican held up a finger. "Number one. Do you believe that Pope John has the power to establish the precepts that are contained in his latest bull, that of *Quorumdam exigit*?"

A black-robed figure stood up at the table, an open book in his arm, his finger held to a certain spot. Fabrizio guessed he was ready to read from the bull, if asked.

Nobilus held up another finger. "And number two. Will you obey the precepts contained in that bull? That is all. Two things. Do you believe and will you obey?"

No one spoke. No one moved in the room below.

Fabrizio's thoughts spun in his head. He did not know what this latest bull contained. He tried to stay away from such theological quarrels. But he knew from the sound of it, that this was a challenge of the highest degree. He looked again to Kerstan and the Guardian. The Guardian stepped closer to the lattice and squinted through the openings. Kerstan's eyes were wide. His pencil hovered, waiting.

Venedictos stepped back, momentary bewilderment passed over his face, swallowed by fierce resolution. "We will answer your questions, Nobilus," he said. "But first you must listen to who we are and why we have done what we have done."

Nobilus stared at him, shaking his head from side to side. Slowly. Deliberately.

Fabrizio didn't want to hear any more. The defiance of the Spirituals made him angry. The presence of Sereno made him sick. He stood up, nodded to his brothers, opened the chestnut door, and swiftly passed through it.

HE LONGED for physical work to do, like drawing water or

pitching hay, something that his taut muscles could find relief in doing while his mind grappled with what he had just seen and heard. Why on earth had Sereno—brilliant, capable Sereno—joined these rigorists who roamed from town to town, mocking the work of other friars?

But it was Fabrizio's turn to pray for those who had made the trip up the hill from Armonia with specific requests, something he usually loved doing. When he entered the chapel doors, a small group was already waiting for him, pain apparent on each face.

He took his seat at the little desk in the room off the main chapel. It was a plain room, small and square, its walls and ceiling painted white, its tile floor the color of earth. Besides the small table, the only things in the room were the chair he sat in, the chair across the table for the supplicants, and a large wooden bucket on the floor behind him. The bucket caught the water that dripped from the ceiling during every rainstorm.

A young woman came first, her hair and neck covered with pale linen, her gown the color of blue that so many women in town wore.

"Brother Fabrizio, my husband is so ill. He has been sick for weeks. Quintus and Cantor have come to see him many times and each time he is helped, but still he is weak. He is not himself. If you could have seen what he was months ago..."

She wiped her eyes with a square of linen. "God alone can help him. Please, Brother Fabrizio, beg God to help me!"

He shed the tension from the council room as he prayed aloud—first, the Latin prayer for the sick, then the words that came to him, words in the language they all used daily and could easily understand. When he had finished, he spoke words from Scripture that had pushed their way into his mind.

"Take this from the psalm, dear woman. *The Lord will fulfill his purpose for me; your love, O Lord, endures forever. Do not abandon the works of your hands.*"

After her, a gray-haired man limped in, leaning heavily on his cane. Tears wet his cheeks before he even sat down. "My daughter, my Angela. She has run away. We have asked everyone, gone everywhere, and we cannot find her."

Fabrizio, filled with the man's grief, prayed as he had for the woman. First in Latin, the language of the Church, followed by a prayer in the people's language. Again he chose a verse from Scripture for the man to hear and take home with him.

A workman, sun-browned and sinewy, rested his injured arm on the small desk. The jagged lines of the wounds flamed a moist, angry red. Fabrizio's stomach tightened at the sight of it.

"We were harvesting rye in the fields west of town," the man said. "As we sat on the ground for supper, wild dogs attacked us. We beat them off and killed one of them, but it was not easy."

"I heard of wild dogs in the area. I was hoping it was just a rumor."

The man held up his arm. "No rumor did this."

Fabrizio walked him to the infirmary after prayer, then returned to the chapel room.

A richly-dressed man waited in the chair, picking nervously at the edge of his mantle. "My son needs a wife," he said. "I wouldn't have come, but..." He looked away quickly. "Well, the need is great."

Fabrizio did not question him, but just nodded. The man looked relieved as he bent his head for prayer.

The last man waiting was as poor as the previous had been rich. His face was thin and pinched and Fabrizio wondered how long he had been hungry.

"The family we worked for in town has moved away. I do not know where to go to find work now. These are hard times and I—I have no skills. I ask from door to door, but they look at me and turn away. You know the saying. It is true. 'No one in poor clothing is honorably treated.' My wife and son—I do not want them to starve."

Fabrizio could feel the man's desperation in his own heart. Tears pricked his eyes. Is this what his own father had looked like? Had he too thought of his wife and son before hopelessness took him? Fabrizio bowed his head and prayed long. Then he took the man to the walkway between the chapel and the library and handed him a broom.

"Here. Let me see you sweep this."

The man looked startled, but took the broom and swept the blown dust off the tiles as Fabrizio watched.

"That is good," said Fabrizio. "Continue on as you are, please. I will be right back."

He hurried to the library building and down the hall to the room next to the Guardian's study where Donatello worked. If he told Donatello about the man's poverty, the procurator would surely give the man a few coins to meet his pressing needs.

The Guardian's office was empty. He and Kerstan were

probably still in the gallery watching the questioning of the Spirituals. Donatello's room was also empty. Fabrizio looked out the hall window into the friary courtyard. No one was in sight. He had seen Donatello's horse earlier in the stables. He must be somewhere. The poor man would be finished with his sweeping soon and must not leave the friary empty-handed.

Fabrizio went back to Donatello's room. There on a polished wood tray sat the small chest of money that Donatello used for desperate need. The key rested in the lock. Fabrizio grabbed the tray and walked quickly down the corridor.

The poor man had finished and was waiting for him. He looked puzzled when he saw Fabrizio bearing the tray.

"Turn the key and take out a five coin and a ten coin."

The man's face lit up. He did exactly what Fabrizio told him to do, showed him the coins he had in his hand, then turned the key to lock the chest again.

"God is already answering your prayers," Fabrizio said to the man. "See, here is a beginning, and God will keep answering. Bring your family to eat meals here. You will not starve." As he said the words, his eyes filled with tears again.

"Thank you, good friar. Thank you!" The man bowed his head and hurried off, the coins firmly clasped in his hand, a look of hope on his face. Fabrizio took a deep breath. He would tell Donatello the exact count and what he had done. Donatello would understand.

He heard the squeak of a door and a stifled cry behind him. Gasps. Then the quick Latin words used to ward off a curse.

Fabrizio turned to find the entire group of Spirituals standing at the library entrance gaping at him. The ques-

tioning must have stopped for the midday meal and Venedictos, Sereno, the hungry youth, and the three others stared at
him. Then their gaze dropped pointedly to the money chest
that rested on the tray in his hands.

What had they seen? Or what did they think they
had seen?

He had not actually touched the money, but it did not
matter. To them he looked like a man who, contrary to his
Franciscan vows, fingered money, used money, possessed
money. To them Fabrizio represented all that was sick in the
Franciscan order. Contempt radiated from every line in their
faces. And from Sereno's just like the others.

6

The Guardian wore the same solemn expression he had worn in the council room's gallery. Donatello had set the tray with the money chest on the Guardian's desk. The coins slid deftly through the procurator's hands and clinked into the chest as he counted each one. Fabrizio's heart pounded as his glance darted from face to face.

"It is just as he said," Donatello announced, as the last coin fell from his hand. "The amount is exact."

"Of course it is just as he said," the Guardian replied. "I did not expect it to be otherwise."

Donatello flushed and glanced apologetically at Fabrizio. "I didn't mean to accuse. You know it is my job to count the money and give an account to my father. He would be here himself, but for his bad leg."

"I am truly sorry, Donatello, and truly sorry, my Guardian." Fabrizio struggled to find the right words to say.

"The man was so desperate. I wanted to give him hope. I swear I touched not one coin."

"Do not be tempted to swear, Fabrizio. I believe you," said the Guardian.

"His clothes were so ragged; the tears were not patched. And he said, he said—" Fabrizio looked down and rubbed his hands together. He could not bring himself to say the proverb, so he hid his feelings in the Latin version. "He said, *In vili veste nemo tractator honeste.*"

The Guardian's expression changed from solemnity to sadness. "That was your mother's proverb. The one she said when she scrubbed your face and combed your hair. 'No one in poor clothing is honorably treated.' She tried hard, hoping people would look past that and see her son."

Fabrizio nodded, grateful that the Guardian remembered. Grateful that he did not have to try to explain.

"Did I do wrong?" Fabrizio asked. "Was this sin?" There. The question was out.

Donatello excused himself, taking the money box back to his room. The Guardian motioned for Fabrizio to sit down in the chair across the desk from him. He waited until Donatello had closed the door behind him before he began to speak.

"Did you sin? I do not think so. You gave money to a poor man. You were not buying or selling. I do not think it was wrong in itself, but it was unwise. Especially in light of the challenging guests among us."

Fabrizio knew that tone of gentle, but firm correction well. How often had he heard it over the years!

The Guardian leaned back in his chair and studied Fabrizio. "You could have waited for Donatello, or asked the man to return the next day and Donatello could have given him the gift."

"But he had just done the work, and you know it is not right for workmen to wait for their pay. You have said so yourself."

Fabrizio knew this was a childish response. He had purposely avoided the main point and picked at a barely related detail instead. He felt ashamed of the words the minute he spoke them.

"I know, Fabrizio. I know." The Guardian nodded graciously. "But to the Spiritual friars, it looked as if you were hiring a man and paying a man, something a Franciscan cannot do.

"And I refer to the Spirituals with caution. We know they already disagree with our way of life here. They see our actions and interpret them as they will. We cannot change that. But we need to be prudent if we are to make it through this trial.

"You could have asked Donatello to give the man a small job, asked first to see if there was room in the accounts for another helper. That would have been of greater benefit to the man than a few minutes sweeping."

Fabrizio dropped his gaze and stared at the grooves in the worn desktop. "I did not think of that," he said.

"It is hard to think," said the Guardian kindly, "when your past is thrust before you. Yet that is the time we must think the most."

⁓

Fabrizio took the herd out to a lowland pasture that afternoon. As the goats gleefully tore the bark from wild olive trees, he tried to forget the looks on the Spirituals' faces. To wipe them out of his mind. But he failed. Their accusing eyes haunted him. *You are not one of us,* they seemed to say. *And we will cast you out.*

It was a look Fabrizio had seen so often in his childhood. Good, clean townspeople so afraid of the dirty, poor boy. His only defense had been to show disdain right back. But disdain could not heal the hurt. And the ache was still a hollow, painful thing inside of him.

Here, in San Stigliano, he had found a home. Here, he had been welcomed to a community. And yet today, inside the precious friary walls, in his own home, he had seen that look again. That separating, dividing look. The look of rejection.

He ate in the kitchen with Gustave, Leo, and the other kitchen boys. But he did not talk much, even with Gustave, as, after the meal, they squeezed the whey from the curds and hung fresh cheeses to dry.

Gustave did not seem to notice. He was more concerned about the unexpected gift of sausage a farmer had just delivered to the friary. Wiping his hands on his apron, he pointed at the pile of links on the worktable in front of him.

"I know I have skill in cooking, Fabrizio, but a Franciscan cook does not have much experience with sausage. I am afraid I will cook it wrong. And that will not please our guests."

"I cannot help you," Fabrizio replied. He didn't feel in the mood to even care about pleasing guests.

Gustave turned one of the links over and a sudden thought lit up his face. "I will boil all of it," he declared. "When the skins split open, and the insides come out, then I will know that it is done."

He looked at Fabrizio for approval and Fabrizio struggled to find something to say.

"I'm sure that will work," he said at last. "I'm sure you know what is best to do."

Gustave seemed pleased with that response.

BECAUSE OF THE presence of contentious guests in the halls of their dormitory, the friars of San Stigliano gathered in the kitchen instead to talk about the day, both helping and interfering with clean-up after the evening meal. Fabrizio rubbed the work tables with a rag, grateful to see that tonight the attention was on Kerstan and not on himself. Everyone wanted to know about the day's inquisition.

"Both sides said what we expected they would say." Kerstan's voice was tired. "They, each of them, hold the correct opinions on obedience to Christ and the Church, and on the poverty that Saint Francis taught. But Nobilus is insisting that they recognize the pope's authority—"

"Well of course!" said Emilian.

"—and agree to obey his recent bull. That is all he is asking them to do."

"What they *must* do, you mean," said Cantor.

Kerstan nodded wearily. "Yes."

"If they only talked about those two things, what took so long?" asked Emilian.

Fabrizio wondered the same.

"Titus persuaded Nobilus to listen to the Spirituals' concerns before insisting on their agreement," said Kerstan. "Nobilus did not want to listen, but he did. Somewhat. That's when the worst of the arguments began."

Kerstan shook his head at the memory. "For a brief time, Titus and Sereno led the discussion back and forth, and I had hope that some good could come from it. But Nobilus was too impatient and took over. So, Venedictos leapt to his feet in response and the arguing began all over again."

Sereno. Kerstan had used the name Sereno. Fabrizio could have no doubt now that it was he. For years he had looked forward to seeing Sereno again. Now, just hearing his name gave him pain.

"So what do we do?" asked Emilian. "What *can* we do?"

"What we've already been given to do," said Kerstan, "and pray and wait."

Benefice nudged a bowl at Fabrizio, startling him and pulling his attention away from the main group. "Some scraps for your goats. It isn't much."

Fabrizio responded with a slight smile. "Any goats who depend on a community of poor friars learn not to expect much."

But he was glad for the excuse to set down his rag, pick up his small lantern, and leave the kitchen, bearing the bowl across the open square to the stables. The servants of the Dominicans were nearby, tending to their horses. He bowed a greeting at them, then ducked into the side where Ermentrude and her friends waited.

"Here, my girls," he said, dumping the scraps into the wooden box that served as a manger and bore many scratches made by goat teeth. He pulled up his milking stool and sat on it as they poked through his offering. Some tasted and ate. Others, as usual, refused.

"Tomorrow we will go up into the hills, I promise. I will need the trip as much as you do, my sisters."

He rubbed his eyes and fell silent. The goats had enough fresh water. He had seen to that before supper. His work for the day was almost over. One by one, as they finished poking through the manger they came over to him, pushing their moist noses into his hands or pressing against him for his caresses. Once they had their share, they found places to curl up in the straw. Fabrizio stayed in the near darkness, thinking.

We do what we've already been given to do, Kerstan had said, *and pray and wait.* But Kerstan did not know any of these poor friars. They were an academic problem to him, a long recording task, a challenge in words and theology.

But what if Kerstan had once admired someone, almost idolized someone, and then, years later, found himself looked down on by that someone. Almost despised by him. Then Kerstan would feel what Fabrizio was feeling now.

A bell rang out in the darkness, melodic and lovely —Benefice in the campanile announcing the hour of Compline. Fabrizio slid to his knees in the matted straw and began to say his nightly prayers.

He STAYED on his knees long after the prayers were over and

the peals of the bell forgotten. He stayed lifting up his heart to the Lord God, begging Him for wisdom and understanding. When the words gave out, he stayed in silence holding up his hurt and confusion to the Lord of the Universe, to Christ his Redeemer.

At last he rubbed his eyes again, crossed himself, and got to his feet. He picked up the lantern and held it up for a last look at the sleeping goats—goats without anger or debates —curled up next to their kin, in short coats and long, indulging in peaceful slumber. As he turned to go, he stopped short and lifted the lantern higher.

A figure stood in the entrance to the goat pen, the shadowy outline of a man, with glinting eyes.

7

———

"**I** remember in my youth a hard-working boy," the figure said. "He weeded the garden rows on his hands and knees, squinting in the twilight late on a summer's eve. When I went to sleep, he was still weeding." The glitter of eyes peered into the dimness. "It *is* you, Fabrizio, isn't it? At first, I thought I might be mistaken."

"I worked hard to keep my mother from starving," Fabrizio answered defensively. "But I worked in vain."

"Your mother starved? To her death?" Sudden concern was in the voice.

Fabrizio could not trust it. He had seen a very different Sereno earlier that day. His own words came stiffly, awkwardly. "The winter sickness carries off the thin ones first. It was after you went away to school."

"But how? How could that happen?"

"The old cook left. The new one had her own family to help. They did not need me any more. It was begging or death. So we begged, but death came anyway."

Sereno crossed himself. "I am so very sorry, Fabrizio. So sorry."

Fabrizio pushed the memories away. He could not bear them, could never bear them. Best to talk of something else. "There is the milking stool if you wish to sit down."

"Thank you." Sereno came all the way in and sat down.

Fabrizio remained standing for a moment, very aware of Sereno's bare feet and the sandals on his own. He hung the small lantern on a post and sat down awkwardly in the straw, covering his sandals with the skirt of his robe.

"What do you need from me, Sereno? Why are you here when the rest of your company are preparing to sleep?"

He had imagined many times what he would say, what he would do, if he ever saw Sereno again. This was not how he imagined it. These words, his old friend, his own mind—all felt foreign to him.

"I came to talk with you," Sereno replied. "Will you not speak with me, Fabrizio? Isn't that what we have been summoned here for? To talk, to converse, to listen?"

Fabrizio could not look at him, but kept his eyes on the dark corner where the goats lay sleeping. The sounds of snuffly breathing rising and falling steadied him. Calmed him.

The look Sereno had given him in the chapel walkway, was it not similar to the look he had given Sereno when he pulled away from him in the dining hall? Did they not, each of them, need to repent?

"I will listen," he said. But his words and his manner were cautious.

Sereno took a deep breath and let it out slowly. "Do you find it curious that we lived in the same village as boys and both grew up and became friars? We haven't seen each other for over ten years at least. " The words came a little slowly, as if they were being carefully chosen.

"At least," Fabrizio repeated.

"And to find you living here." There was something behind the tone in which Sereno said this, a disappointment, a barely concealed disapproval.

"I am a Franciscan," Fabrizio replied boldly. "Where else would I be living?"

Sereno frowned. "Saint Francis would have a different idea than this."

"So, you have come to attack my life now?"

"I? It is you who are attacking mine!" Sereno shot back.

Fabrizio stared at him. "I attack you? What have I ever done to you, Sereno?"

A hostile silence fell between them. Sereno took another deep breath, his eyes on the matted straw at his feet. "No, not you, Fabrizio," his voice was calm again. "It is the church authorities who will not understand. Who attack." He glanced at Fabrizio. "I have been foolish. I did not listen to you first. I have spoken without hearing."

"Very well, since you invite me to, I will speak," said Fabrizio. "We are both Franciscans, you and I. We have both taken the vows of poverty, chastity, and obedience. We build our lives on simplicity, humility, and prayer. My cell in the dormitory is just as spare as the one you are sleeping in. Yet, you demand I must be even poorer.

"How poor must I be? If I am too poor, I cannot *help* the poor! If I were as you are now, you would not have had your dinner tonight. I am God's answer to your prayer for food, yet you disapprove of me for that?"

Sereno shook his head. "We are to depend on God, not what we can do."

"He gives us things to do. Should I purposefully *not* do them? This would honor Him more than the doing?"

"It is so easy to depend on the work of our hands, to let it take the place of God."

"But surely that is the fault of our hearts, not the fault of our hands."

One of the goats stirred restlessly, bleating weakly.

Sereno lowered his voice. "God has given me this to do: To trust Him with my whole self. To walk the land and speak of Him to others. To pray for them and preach to them wherever they are, in their fields, on the roads. People give us things and what we don't use we give away to others by the end of the day. They trust us to bless others. They open their homes or barns or churches for us to sleep in when night comes."

Fabrizio leaned forward. "And I praise God by feeding the goats He has made, by milking them, by tending His creation. By loving the animals as Saint Francis did. And by praying for all the people."

For the first time a note of confusion entered Sereno's voice. "Yes, you do."

Then he spoke with more conviction. "But you own things—the buildings, the walls, the gates, the books, the tiled roofs and floors. The goats! And you promised to be poor. You made a *vow* to be poor!"

"You speak of what you do not understand, Sereno. No one can own a goat. A goat responds to a man by agreement only—the goat's agreement."

Sereno gave a short laugh, but no pleasure sounded in it.

Fabrizio went on. "The buildings you see around you

were a gift also, a gift to the friars from the last man in a line of humble gentry. He sold off all his land and gave the buildings to the Church in his will.

"We are here by grace alone, for you know that all such property belongs to the pope. Our procurator uses the small money that comes our way to feed us and others, to feed with bread and with the Word of God."

Sereno shook his head, as if to shake away all the words Fabrizio had just said. "Do you not see? Your habit of life is blinding you to what it has become! The worldliness has crept into your community making you betray the vows you took to the Franciscan Order."

Fabrizio stared at him, stunned. "What? Where? How am I blind? We have not betrayed the Order! Saint Francis himself was given a mountain and he accepted it. And we do the work of God every single day."

He remembered Venedictos' sharp answer to the Guardian at noontime prayers, the day the Spirituals had arrived. What had he said? Something about Christ having no pillow.

"The pillow on my bed, does that bother you, Sereno? Am I to feel guilty for putting my head on a pillow at night? If I remove the pillow from my bed, am I somehow holier? Does holiness in life depend on the placement of a pillow? Did our Lord Jesus suffer on the cross for pillows?"

"We are to share in Christ's poverty," Sereno replied, speaking each word distinctly. "When we feel His poverty, we become more like Him. And He had no pillow on which to lay His head." Sereno finished coldly, the sound of Venedictos in his voice.

"Our Lord laid His head on the ground which He had

made," said Fabrizio. "He lived as owning nothing, yet every-thing belonged to Him because He had brought all of it into being!"

Sereno did not answer for a few moments. He had turned away, and Fabrizio could not see any part of his face. When he spoke again, his voice cut like a knife.

"Perhaps you are the one who should advise the pope on the writing of his next bull. He and Nobilus both would be grateful for your help in crushing the Spirituals."

The sarcasm hurt. Especially since Sereno had always known that Fabrizio was not very clever.

"I am not a theologian," he answered, trying hard to keep his voice even. "And I do not want to crush anyone. It is you who refuse to acknowledge me as your Franciscan brother. Very well. We do not agree. Therefore, we are not brothers." Without looking at Sereno, he got to his feet, took the lantern, and left the goat pen.

As he crossed the square, a wave of guilt at his abrupt departure washed over him. He shoved it aside. The moon was out. The stars were out. Sereno would have no trouble seeing his way back to the dormitory in the dark.

8

As Fabrizio had promised, he took the goats high up into the hills for the whole of the next day. Old Leonard was among his sheep and waved at them as they climbed. On they went, Ermentrude leading and Lily watchful at the end, while the sun rose higher in the sky.

They stopped first near a mountain stream. The goats wandered happily, sampling the coarse grasses, the thistles and wildflowers, and stripping the trees of bark. From time to time they chased each other across the hillside, and often leapt into the air for the sheer joy of it.

Fabrizio felt no such joy, though he welcomed the solitude. He found a good spot on the stream bank, took off his sandals and plunged his feet into the cold water for a few moments. Thus refreshed, he pulled out the rye loaf and the boiled eggs that Gustave had packed for him.

He longed to pray something more than all the prayers he had memorized. No words came to mind, but these: *Lord, have mercy.* He prayed his psalms at the proper hours and silently held up his heart to God in between times, walking among the goats with his staff in hand.

They spent the day rambling through the hills, the goats eagerly discovering new sources of food. Once, in her fervor to tear off the bark of a scrub oak tree, Sancha caught her horns in its low branches. Fabrizio spoke gently to the panicked goat, took her head in his hands, and guided it to freedom, though the rough tree bark tore his robe.

As the afternoon lengthened, they began their descent. Smoke rose from some hidden field down in the valley. Fabrizio heard the distant sound of the Vesper bell long before he was ready to leave the hills. Nevertheless, he gathered the goats for the remaining downward journey and prayed aloud as they walked, Ermentrude appearing to listen as she trotted by his side.

The campanile roof came into view first as always, followed by the chapel roof and the others, but for the first time, the sight of his home brought no happiness to him. He returned the goats to their pen in the stables, then set about the task of milking them. He took his time.

They had stayed so long in the hills that he had missed dinner. That was all right. There was solace in being alone with the animals. It seemed that the milk pails were filled too soon, and he could not keep from taking them to Gustave.

As he crossed the square toward the kitchen, he saw Prentice the scrivener sitting in the evening dusk, under the large oak in the center of the square. Prentice was leaning against the trunk of the tree, his long legs stretched out before him, apparently enjoying the peaceful end of the day.

Fabrizio greeted him, then asked, "And how far did you get in the sacred letter today?"

Prentice tilted his head up as if he were studying the sky, then said, "*They are senseless, faithless, heartless, ruthless.*"

"That's a hard passage to end on," said Fabrizio. "And Saint Paul was speaking of...?"

"Godless men," Prentice answered. "We're almost to the end of the first chapter."

"Ah," said Fabrizio, turning toward the kitchen door. "A good day's work then."

"And the copy looks beautiful!" said Prentice, a proud smile on his face.

THE FRIARS HAD GATHERED AGAIN in the kitchen after dinner and were deep in conversation when Fabrizio brought in the last pails of milk. Gustave placed a full bowl in front of him and Fabrizio sat down and picked up his spoon. Then stopped.

Blobs of gray, ragged meat floated in the bowl, mangled sausages, spilling from their skins. Was this what the company pot contained? Fabrizio motioned to Gustave.

"Wrong bowl," he whispered.

Gustave shook his head at his own mistake, took the bowl and filled a new one for Fabrizio. Fabrizio sniffed it and smiled. Garden potage, to which Gustave had been generous with the fennel. Nothing eased the pain of an empty stomach like fennel. After several spoonfuls, Fabrizio raised his head to look around at his brothers.

Emilian leaned against the long wooden worktable, his fingers tapped continually on its surface. Kerstan, on a stool nearby, rubbed his forehead with the palm of one hand.

Benefice's expression was placid as he washed the wooden bowls. Cantor's showed his usual wryness as he stood near the others, watching them closely. Donatello, in a brilliant blue mantle, stood near the dining room door, looking grim.

Emilian was asking the question, "Who speaks for the Spirituals?" He, more than many of them, took great interest in the actual process of the debates.

"Only three," Kerstan replied. "Venedictos most often. Then Lucien and Sereno. Sereno is by far the most easy to listen to and I think the Dominicans prefer him over Venedictos, although all the poor ones are equally stubborn."

"And who speaks for the Dominicans?" said Emilian.

"Nobilus. Always, Nobilus. Titus began to address them once, but Nobilus took over before his argument was fully developed. It might have been because Titus was not forceful enough." Kerstan looked thoughtful. "I would like to hear Titus and Sereno discuss for a time, but I do not think their leaders would allow it."

"Were there no breakthroughs, then? No real progress?" asked Donatello. "Nothing good to report to my father?"

Kerstan shook his head from side to side. "Nothing that I could distinguish."

"So it's like a river then," said Cantor.

The conversation stumbled into a confused silence. "A river?" said Emilian, irritated.

"Yes," said Cantor. "Like this: the words like water flow through the same channels again and again, but this river will not flood its banks. Instead, it makes deeper and deeper grooves in the earth, and covers no new ground no matter how great the flow."

The friars considered this silently while Fabrizio drank

his soup. He was too tired to follow Cantor's thinking, and was glad not to be part of the conversation.

"Sadly, yes," Kerstan agreed. "It seems like that."

"And our future may depend on such a debate," muttered Emilian.

"Certainly theirs does," Kerstan replied.

"How much longer will this go on, I wonder," said Cantor.

And no one answered him this time.

THE ANSWER to Cantor's question came late the following week, after more weary days of arguing between the Spirituals and the Dominicans. Nobilus had clearly lost track of the two original questions he had insisted on, and debate ensued over what seemed like every word in the papal bulls and the work of Franciscan writers. Passionate discussions moved from the council room into the library, where both Nobilus and Venedictos pushed Prentice and the scriveners aside and assaulted the Scriptures themselves with linen gloves.

The arguing drove the scholars from their studies, the doves from their rooftop perches, and the Guardian from his office to the chapel for long hours of prayer. Visitors to San Stigliano felt the tension within its walls. The people who used to come freely hurried away now, leaving their deliveries, prayer requests, and absolved sins behind them. The friars that could leave fled the friary and spent their days in town, preaching, teaching, working, and praying.

Fabrizio took the goats to the hills every day that he was not required to remain for prayers or confessions or cleaning or cheese-making. He had seen Sereno only briefly since the night of their argument in the goat pen. And at those times, Sereno had always been with his fellows on the opposite end of the chapel or at the far end of the dining hall, never alone. For his part, Fabrizio had always been too busy in whatever he was doing to pause whenever the Spirituals walked nearby. And he always let Leo or the silent server take the cheese to the Spirituals' table at meals.

After a day in the hills, he was eating dinner late again, listening to the now-expected conversation in the kitchen. Donatello sat musing, a troubled look on his face, while the friars washed dishes and swept floors, clearing the way between one day's work and the next. Kerstan, too, entered late and the haggard look on his face immediately drew everyone's attention.

"A final decree has come," he announced, his voice breaking a little as he said the words. "Cardinal Scantoni sent it to Nobilus. I have seen it. And copied it. It—it carries the pope's approval." He rested both his hands on the worn work-table, as if to steady himself.

"Unless the Spiritual friars accept the authority of the pope, recant their position, and unite again with other Franciscans—"

Kerstan swallowed hard.

"They are never to leave San Stigliano."

9

Cantor, Benefice, and Emilian all started to say something at the same time, then stopped. Gustave quickly called to the serving boys, shoved loaves of bread in their hands, and sent them out the door towards home. The attention turned back to Kerstan.

"Why on earth?" said Emilian, fingers clutching his broom handle. "What happened to make him decree such a thing?"

Kerstan sank onto a stool like one sinking beneath a heavy weight. "Venedictos claimed that the Spirituals were indeed obeying the pope. They were obeying Pope Celestine's declaration.

"Nobilus told him that had been changed and that Venedictos knew well that it had changed. Venedictos responded by saying, 'But how can it be changed unless the one who changed it acted heretically?'"

Gasps sounded in the room. A wooden bowl slid from

Benefice's grasp and bounced from the tabletop to the floor, startling everyone.

Emilian was the first to speak. "He accused a pope of heresy?"

Fabrizio lowered his spoon, ignoring the last bites of his soup, and waited for Kerstan to answer.

Kerstan nodded slowly, wearily. "I—I do not know if that is what Venedictos really meant, but Nobilus thought it was. Nobilus struck him in the face. Then he swore that the Spirituals would never leave this friary again unless they repented and accepted Pope John as their master."

The brothers looked one to another, bewilderment on their faces. Kerstan sighed and shook his head. "They'll never do it. I have heard them day after day. They will never recant."

Nobilus struck the Spiritual leader? Fabrizio gaped at Kerstan. Had the blow been a hard one? And who had helped Venedictos after Nobilus had struck him?

"Wait a minute." Cantor looked confused. "You said Nobilus ordered them to stay here as a result of Venedictos' argument. Yet he already had the document from the Cardinal. They must have planned this."

"Yes," said Kerstan. "I had thought of that."

"We will become a prison then," said Emilian. "We will have to keep the gates shut and locked, and post guard by each of their rooms."

"We cannot afford to become a prison." Donatello stepped forward, his face an angry red. "We cannot keep feeding the inquisitors and the rebels and still repair the chapel roof, not even if we sell every one of Fabrizio's goats."

"We can't sell the goats," said Fabrizio. But he said it softly and no one paid him heed.

"If we all become like our poor brothers, then we won't have to pay for anything," said Cantor, in his light mocking way.

Emilian turned on him. "Be quiet, Cantor! For once, be quiet!"

Gustave stopped wiping the tables and held up the rag, gesturing with it. "The poor ones barely eat anything, barely cost anything, yet they rebel. The Dominicans are obedient, yet eat much more. Perhaps we should ask the Guardian about this. He..." His voice dropped, and he stared past them to the doorway.

The group turned quickly to see their Guardian standing there, his eyes studying them sadly. By the look on his face, Fabrizio knew he had heard every word. Seen the results of frustration among them. Several heads bowed in repentant shame.

Yet, when the Guardian spoke, it was Gustave he answered. "Men's minds are difficult enough to understand, and now you want me to explain their stomachs?"

Gustave laughed, and Cantor joined him. The atmosphere in the room lightened. Emilian raised his head again.

"Though you may have handled it poorly," the Guardian continued, "you are correct on one thing. This decree is very serious. I have written of it to our *Custode*. You may have seen his messenger's horse in the square.

"This new trial will test our wisdom even more, for we do not know what lies ahead of any of us. We must be ever careful of how we act toward the poor ones, the inquisitors, and each other."

Fabrizio thought of his mistake with the money chest. The Guardian, out of grace, was not looking at him.

The Guardian went on. "Always remember that San Stigliano does not belong to us, whatever happens here. We are indeed poor friars who only have it on loan. It is God's. We will do His work within these walls and outside of them as well. This is a place to work from, not for."

Fabrizio's mind raced back to the decree, and the picture of an imprisoned Sereno. "But, dear Guardian," he rose from his stool at the far end of the room. "What of this demand? How are we to be the jailers of these Spirituals?"

The Guardian smiled gently at Fabrizio, and Fabrizio took heart.

"My dear Fabrizio, dear brothers all," he said, turning to look at everyone in the room. "Franciscans do not take vows to become jailers."

Relief shone on their faces, and Fabrizio felt the rush of it inside. They all knew what the Guardian meant. They too had vows their souls must keep, vows of chastity, obedience, and poverty. Nowhere had they ever pledged to bind another man.

Donatello spoke. "The inquisitors could use civic authorities for jailers."

The relief disappeared.

"Surely not on Church property!" Kerstan cried.

"I have written to the *Custode*," the Guardian repeated firmly.

Emilian stepped forward, still holding his broom. "Dear

Guardian, please answer me for all of us. Are these self-appointed Spirituals heretics?" He said the last word cautiously, carefully, as if it were dangerous even to say it. "I mean, is what they're saying and doing heretical? They have accused a pope of heresy, but aren't they themselves guilty of it?"

All eyes went immediately to the Guardian. All ears ready to hear. Eternity itself, seemed to wait for the answer.

The Guardian turned to the cook. "Gustave, may I have a stool, please? Thank you." Their gray-haired leader sat down and looked at them, and in his eye was that keen intelligence Fabrizio admired. If anyone had the answer to this, the Guardian would. Fabrizio slid back onto his own stool to listen.

"Heresy," the Guardian began, "is a word that strikes terror into a heart. It is one thing believers fear greatly, and there is good reason for that. Heresy twists the truth of God, until people are following it instead of God Himself. We *should* fear it.

"However, because of that fear, people are quick to accuse, to name any disagreement 'heresy!' We must not race to do so, but we must examine things very carefully."

He nodded at Emilian. "As you know, heresy has disobedience in it. But not all disobedience is heresy, although disobedience is serious enough and must be addressed.

"Heresy involves believing things about God that are incorrect. But is every incorrect thought heresy? No. Incorrect thoughts often arise on the path our minds take as they grow up in the faith. Unfortunately, it is often man's nature to be incorrect."

The Guardian stopped speaking, covered his mouth with his hand, and began to cough. Gustave quickly handed him a cup of ale. The Guardian nodded his thanks and took a mouthful.

"Here, Fabrizio. I forgot yours," Gustave whispered, setting another cup on the table near him.

"Thank you," Fabrizio whispered back.

The Guardian cleared his throat and continued.

"So what is heresy? It is when a person takes the core doctrines of Christianity and twists them. Changes them. Important doctrines such as the death of Christ for sinners. His powerful resurrection. The nature of the Triune God.

"A heretic would change these while claiming to speak for God! And he would refuse to repent even when his falseness is proven by the Word of God.

"Heresy is cruel. It keeps people from God, now and forever. Because of this, the church *must* root out heresies."

Fabrizio quietly stirred the last of the broth in his bowl, watching the liquid as it swirled around his spoon. He felt uneasy. Sereno could not be a *heretic*, could he? For some reason, Fabrizio could not believe that.

"Now," the Guardian turned on his stool to face Emilian, "to answer your question directly. These Spirituals challenge our practices, yes, but they have not tried to change any of our doctrines, at least Venedictos and his band have not. I do not know about all the others. I have read Kerstan's notes and listened to the debates myself. So far, I have found nothing to give doctrinal alarm."

"But the Spirituals are disobedient, aren't they?" Emilian asked. "Otherwise the Dominicans would not be here."

The Guardian nodded slowly and, Fabrizio thought, somewhat reluctantly. "The pope has given orders which they will not obey, so yes, we must say that they are disobedient. Here we come to the danger.

"If the pope can gather a decision from his cardinals that to disobey this recent bull *is* an act of heresy, then I fear what will become of these Spirituals."

Fabrizio felt a stab of fear with these words, and immediately tried to argue it away. *What could happen?* Kerstan had hinted of grim things in other parts of the world. In far-away Provence, or south of Rome. Surely nothing awful could happen here. Nothing!

But the Guardian looked so serious. He must be thinking of something more. That something, whatever it was, made no one rush to ask a question. Even Emilian was silent, waiting.

"I actually came tonight," the Guardian said finally, "to discuss a different sort of danger with you. And that is zeal.

"This friary is filled with passionate guests. You have heard them. I have heard them. Unfortunately, the towns-people have also heard them.

"The zeal to serve God in a particular way is not given to everyone. The Holy Spirit leads one man one way, another man another. He is God. It is His domain. And He understands it best.

"But men are quick to say, 'because I feel this zeal strongly, *you must too.*'" The Guardian lifted both hands into the air and Fabrizio caught a hint of Venedictos in the action.

"'Because I do things this way, *you must too.*'" The Guardian struck his fist on the tabletop. Like Nobilus would have done.

Cantor gave a wry smile at this. Fabrizio knew that only

the seriousness of the topic kept his friend from laughing out loud.

The Guardian became himself again. His quiet, careful, teaching voice flowed around them.

"We know that passion inside a soul is an amazing thing. The strength of it seems to flow from the Giver of Life Himself. Yet here again we must be careful. When Elijah waited on Mt. Horeb for God to speak, he knew that God was not in the fire that came. He knew God was not in the earthquake. Where was God? He was in the words He spoke to His prophet.

"Zeal is not a good teacher. It does not discern. It only feels. And every feeling of ours, just as our every thought, must submit to the Word of God. Here I warn you."

He looked around at them again and Fabrizio had never seen him so serious.

"If you raise any zeal higher than the Word, the wisdom, and the love of God," the Guardian said, "that zeal becomes demonic."

An unexpected word. As fearsome as heresy. Emilian looked as if he wanted to ask another question. Fabrizio hoped he would. There was so much to think through here. He would have to ask Kerstan later.

The Guardian got to his feet and regarded them all intently. "Do you understand what I am saying to you?"

Fabrizio nodded. Of course he understood. How could he not? The Guardian was speaking of the Spirituals. Of Venedictos. Of Sereno. Of their stubborn determination to insist on their own way. And this insistence was destroying the life of San Stigliano.

But the Guardian was still speaking. "I mean *any* zeal. Whether it is for their way of life. Or *ours*."

The Guardian went to the door and Donatello followed him out. Benefice turned back to the sink. Gustave wiped the worktable. Emilian swept the floor with determined strokes. Cantor stirred the fire. Kerstan put his head in his hands. No one spoke. It was as if the Guardian's last words had swept all the air from the room.

Fabrizio stared down into the small remains of his soup. He felt as empty as his bowl.

10

———

Late the next night, after Compline, while the community of friars went to its rooms for sleep and Fabrizio was tucking his goats in for the night, a shadowy figure appeared again at the doorway of the goat pen. Fabrizio did not know why he had come, did not know what to say to him. So saying nothing, he pulled the milking stool from its corner, and set it in the center of the pen.

Sereno stepped in and sat down, also without saying a word. Fabrizio knelt in the fresh straw among his flock, rubbing their heads and backs. Ermentrude leaned heavily against his side, and he was glad of it. She had always been an ally in heart.

For the most part, the goats ignored the stranger. A few looked alarmed at his presence. Two others began to take tentative, curious steps toward him.

When after some time Sereno still had not uttered one word, Fabrizio broke the uneasy silence. "We were told that you will be with us for some time."

Sereno reached his hand out to the most daring goat and ran his fingertips through her tangled coat. The goat took several steps closer. "It seems we are not to leave," he said in a lifeless voice, "without our hearts being wrenched from our bodies."

"I am sorry for you," said Fabrizio. And the words surprised him even as he spoke them. Because for a moment, he had become again the little boy he had once been, concerned about everything that concerned the friend he revered. Then he realized, he truly *was* sorry for Sereno.

"May I ask you something, Sereno?" he said, as he stroked Ermentrude's back. He tried to keep the tone of his words peaceful, so Sereno would hear no threat in them. "There is something I do not understand. May I ask why it is you want to be so very poor?

"I lived with an empty belly much of my life, and I can tell you there is no godliness in it, no sanctity. Before your cook took pity on me and let me work in your garden, there were too many days when we had barely anything to eat. And days we had nothing at all."

Sereno was looking at him. "What did you do?"

"A peasant outside of town did not mind if I sometimes took what his pigs did not want." Fabrizio pulled Ermentrude closer and rubbed her neck, picking out bits of straw from her long coat. "I learned to smile at the wealthy as they sat and ate in the inn yards. They would sometimes give me the last crumbs of their bread or the bites of meat that were too tough to chew. I searched through the trash, though I had to fight the dogs for it. I always lost to the dogs.

"One woman, a traveler, told me I should go to the back

door of all the nice houses and ask for work. I did, and they all said no. Until one day I was at your back door."

"What did our cook tell you?" Sereno asked quietly.

"That I could weed the garden and she would give me the scraps from your dinner table in return. I carried them to my mother in a chipped pottery bowl, only after I swore to the cook I would bring the bowl back the next day. At the end of every week, she gave me a coin. Then she started to give me the clothes you had outgrown. You still are taller than me."

"Where did you live? Where did you sleep?" Sereno's questions held real interest. The lifelessness he had worn when he came in was slipping away.

"Under trees," Fabrizio answered. "Behind buildings. In a goat pen for many years. The farmer was afraid of being robbed, so my mother and I slept inside the entrance to his pen to protect his goats."

"I am sorry, Fabrizio. I never asked you. I never knew."

Fabrizio shrugged. "We were both nine years old. What do young boys know of the world? What can they know beyond their own lives, their own situations?"

The goats had had enough petting. Ermentrude licked his neck, avoiding his beard, her usual good night to him. She pulled away and went to find her place in the straw with her sisters, legs bent, hooves tucked in, heads resting on each others' backs as they preferred, or nestled by themselves near the wall where the straw was thickest. For a moment Fabrizio saw his mother lying in the straw again, his own head resting on her outstretched arm. He pressed his fingers into his eyes.

"I tell you this, Sereno," he said in a low voice. "Every fast day I obey, but in my heart I become a scared, hungry boy again."

He felt Sereno's hand on his shoulder. "The Lord Christ will heal you, Fabrizio."

The tone was gentle, but anger flared inside of Fabrizio —anger from he knew not where—and he threw off the hand. "I don't want healing! I want security. I want provision. And this, this I have. Why do you want to take this from me? You say I am not a good Franciscan. Do I do harm? I work all day so you can eat. Do you despise me for this?"

Sereno picked up a piece of straw and twisted it between his fingers, first one way, then the other.

Fabrizio took a deep breath and let it out with a shudder. "You were secure," he said in a calmer voice. "You had everything—a home, a family, a father. A place where people would look for you, would wait for you. How I wanted to be you! I prayed I could be you."

Sereno gave a rueful smile. "Yes, I had a father. My father disowned me when I became a Franciscan."

Fabrizio remembered his history lessons. "Just like Saint Francis."

"Yes," said Sereno. "Just like Saint Francis."

"Why then did you give it all up? You can be a Franciscan and not starve."

Sereno kept twisting the straw back and forth. "I wanted more, Fabrizio."

Fabrizio stared at him. "Starving is more?"

Sereno shook his head slowly. "Peace. I wanted—I craved —peace." He ran his fingers down the length of the straw piece. Straightening out what he had been twisting.

"My whole life had been shaped by the needs of money. How much this cost, how much that cost, what the expense would be, what the income would be. My father spoke of nothing else but what things meant in terms of money. There was no other consideration. I was already weary of it before I met you. And wondering how I could be free of it."

Fabrizio did not know what to say to this. Could not imagine it.

Sereno looked up at him abruptly. "Do you remember the day when I was to run an errand across town and you were sent to go with me and help carry things for me?"

Fabrizio nodded. It had been one of the few happy days of his childhood. Trailing after Sereno, listening to his chatter, he had felt like a normal boy. He had re-lived that memory over and over for years.

"Do you remember that the street we took led past the friary in town?" Sereno went on. "And there was a tree that grew close to the wall, gnarled and full of limbs?"

Fabrizio took up the story. "And you said we were to set our packages down at the foot of the tree and climb it to look over the wall. I didn't think to ask you why."

"Just curious. No other reason."

"I didn't stop to ask because I was curious too."

Sereno smiled. "I think often about that day. For when I looked over the wall I saw something I had never seen before." They met each other's gaze for the first time, as Fabrizio waited for Sereno to continue.

"It was peace, Fabrizio. As the holy men talked and worked and sang, dressed in simple robes, I saw peace. In that moment I knew what I was to do with my life. When I was old enough, I would join a religious order. I heard Venedictos speak when I was at the university in Bologna, and then I knew that the future I longed for had finally come to me."

Fabrizio winced at the thought of Venedictos influencing his friend. But the memory of that errand day had changed both of them, and this he shared with Sereno forever, no matter what.

"That day in the tree," he confessed, "that day, too, I saw my future before me."

Sereno's eyes widened. "You knew that day you would take holy orders as well?"

"My mind did not, but my heart, my spirit did."

"And what did you see when you looked over the wall?" Sereno spoke with the eagerness of the young boy he had been.

Fabrizio tried to smile in response, but he felt the poignant sadness of the memory. "I saw safety. Freedom from want. The chance to be warm and sheltered. Where night after night you do not have to fear the wolves."

And he had left that fear long ago. Here in this warm stable with its stone walls, tiled roof, and solid doors, here the oil lamp flickered, driving away the dark. A goat murmured in her sleep, a soft, musing bleat. Some of the signs of home. A good home.

"May I take a turn to ask you something now, Fabrizio? There is something *I* do not understand."

Fabrizio glanced up from where he sat in the straw and nodded.

"After such a hard life as yours, what made you take the vows of poverty?"

Fabrizio gave him a wry look, one that he had often seen on Cantor's face. "I already knew destitution. I thought mere poverty would be an improvement."

For a fleeting moment, Sereno smiled. "But there are other holy orders. Why the poor Franciscans?"

Fabrizio's gaze swept the row of sleeping goats, the coats of different colors blending into harmony in the soft light. When he spoke, he spoke seriously and true to his heart.

"I loved the Franciscans because they loved the poor. It was their love that drew me."

An uneasy look passed over Sereno's face. And quickly vanished. "What brought you here, to this friary?" he asked.

It was hard to speak of. Fabrizio hadn't spoken of it for years. But he hadn't spoken of *any* part of his childhood for years, until tonight. To Sereno.

He took a deep breath and fixed his gaze where Ermentrude slept, her eyes closed, her side rising and falling in the peaceful rhythm of slumber.

"My mother died in the night as winter was coming on. I was almost twelve. The next day the owner of the goats was angry that he had a dead woman and a boy on his hands. He had me help him put my mother's body in his cart and ride with him to the quarry outside of town. All the way he talked loud. Angry. This wasn't his fault. Why did he have to deal with this. He could barely afford to buy coffins for his own family. He couldn't spend money on a woman he barely knew. What was he supposed to do?"

"He dumped my mother's body into the quarry. When I saw her fall in, I started walking, then running away. He yelled something after me, but I do not know what it was."

And it all came back to him. The sight of her arms and legs sliding into the pit, like a giant rag doll. The whole world lurched in that moment and never righted itself. A moment that woke him night after night, screaming with the nightmare of it. The Guardian's cool hand on his forehead, murmuring soothing prayers until he fell asleep again.

He wished Ermentrude was at his side instead of sleeping in the straw. How many times had he wrapped his arms around her and cried into her neck at the memory. He blinked rapidly now, lost in the darkness of the past, until he remembered that Sereno still sat quietly, waiting for the rest of the story.

Fabrizio took another deep breath and willed himself the courage to continue.

"I walked from our town up to the next and then beyond. Peasants with wagons gave me rides. 'Where are you headed?' they asked.

"I said whatever came to mind. North. West. Directions I had heard carriage drivers shout. It didn't matter, not to anyone. Except God.

"The last wagon dropped me off in the center of Armonia, this town below us. A woman on the street told me I could get food at the friary. They always have food, she said.

"I came up the hill as a cold wind was blowing. The Guardian saw me waiting at the gate, afraid to come in. Soon I had a seat near the fire and a large bowl of stew in front of me. At that moment, I remembered looking over the friary wall with you. I asked the Guardian if I could stay.

"Someone had just given them a goat, an odd goat, one of a breed that should have horns, but this one didn't." He glanced over at Ermentrude's shaggy coat, her sides lifting and falling with her breath, as she slept with her head close to Sancha's.

"So this goat was given to the friars, and they did not know how to take care of her. But I did. So I stayed. I studied with the Guardian and worked and lived here. The security and provision I had longed for were in San Stigliano waiting for me." He said this last without apology, and wondered if Sereno would challenge it.

"Did you ever go back, Fabrizio? To see—to see...?" Sereno was speaking carefully, but there was compassion in his voice.

Fabrizio nodded. "Two years later the Guardian and Quintus went back with me. We went to the quarry, and the Guardian said a burial service for my mother. The quarry workers did not mind. They thought we were blessing the pit at some patron's request."

He paused a moment, before uttering the last sentence of the story. "I remember many psalms and many prayers and a hymn of such heartbreaking grace and love that I have not been able to sing it since. "

He looked around the pen, at the lantern hanging on its hook, the pitchfork and pail in the corner, the mounds of straw around the sleeping goats. "These walls, this community, it means everything to me."

Sereno said nothing in response. No attack came. And in the silence, Fabrizio felt hope rise in him, hope for Sereno's friendship. After all, Sereno was the only one who had seen anything of his former life. If only Sereno would understand his life now.

Fabrizio wanted to heal the rift that lay between them. To show Sereno that he, Fabrizio, was a Franciscan too, one that Sereno could acknowledge and accept. He began to speak earnestly.

"Sereno, the day you saw me with the money box for the poor sweeper...I didn't touch the money. I couldn't find

Donatello, so I got the money tray from his room. I have told the Guardian—"

"So he tried to explain to us." Sereno sighed. "Fabrizio, one of the many things this friary does not seem to understand is that a Franciscan is not to use money. It is one of the fundamental things about him."

The face of the boyhood friend faded, and as the words flowed, it once again became the hard face of Venedictos' follower, one who found in Fabrizio and his home, evidence of all that was sick in the Franciscan Order.

Fabrizio's heart sank as Sereno went on. "You have a rich benefactor, this Donatello, who provides whatever you wish."

"He is rich, but he is not our benefactor. He serves as procurator in his father's stead, keeping the accounts so we may keep our vows. The popes have provided for this for years."

Fabrizio could tell Sereno more. Could tell him the reason Donatello loved the friary so much. Could tell him that Donatello fell horribly ill as a child and was at the point of death when the Guardian and Quintus prayed for him. Healing had come swift and sure. Everyone knew it had been a miracle. Fabrizio had heard about it during his first weeks at the friary.

He could also tell Sereno that in spite of all this, the Guardian would not let Donatello's family support San Stigliano. They held the office of procurator, yes—handling money people gave and paying out the money for needed supplies—but did little more.

The look on Sereno's face told Fabrizio that it wouldn't matter. Whatever he might say would only be empty explanations. False excuses set forth only to cover the workings of a false heart. After a few moments, Sereno even turned his face away.

Fabrizio couldn't stand this. "What of this rebellious independence you Spirituals are so proud of? Isn't it just as opposed to the Franciscan life as a love for worldly goods? If I *did* love them. Can't you see that I don't? I am a Franciscan just as you are. We have taken the same vows, Sereno. The same vows—"

"Yes, but it looks as if only one of us has kept them!" Sereno glared at him in accusation.

Fabrizio stared back, gaping. This was unbearable.

He stood up quickly before Sereno could speak again, and reached for the lantern. "I must go."

Sereno rose also, but said nothing to him as they walked across the dark square and around the tree toward the dormitory. He did not speak either. They moved swiftly, each aware of the awkwardly painful presence of the other. Side by side again, after all these years, yet divided by everything they cared so deeply about.

Later that night, as he listened to the heavy snore from Emilian's bed and the lighter one from Kerstan's, Fabrizio pressed his face into his small, straw-filled pillow and wept.

11

———

The next morning, layers of low clouds covered the foothills, obscuring the heights and closing in the friary under a white, moist roof.

"You know what these clouds mean, Ermentrude," Fabrizio said, at the early milking. "We cannot go up into the hills today. I cannot see through clouds and what good is a goatherd who cannot see very far? Besides, Gustave needs my help in the kitchen later."

He took the herd to the low pastures around Armonia instead, and wandered the valley with them trying hard to fix his mind on the good of the life he knew. On the faithful friendliness of goats. On the waves and smiles of the people they met in the lanes as they passed. On the joy of good work to do and psalms to pray. And not to think of decrees and threats, accusations and hostility. Of the Spirituals and Sereno.

After a few hours, Fabrizio decided the goats had eaten enough, and herded them back to the friary to rest and chew on what they had been able to find. The clouds had lifted a little, and the sound of children's voices greeted him as he led his goats through the gates. A welcome sound in the midst of all the heaviness that filled the friary now.

Emilian had positioned his class of young sandal-makers on the stone benches which sat between the end of the library building and the gate wall. Each boy had a small length of rope in his hands. Emilian stood before them, holding his own piece of rope in the air as he guided an end through a loop to make a knot, one of the knots necessary for making sandals out of rope.

"Stay here, Ermentrude." Fabrizio left the goats in the middle of the courtyard and waited until his friend had finished his explanation. The boys' eyes turned to him, interested in any interruption.

"Please, excuse me," he began. "I just wanted to thank you, Emilian, for sewing my robe. I found it on the peg this morning, all mended. It must have been your work."

Emilian smiled. "Yes, I did it. It would only take a few moments for me to do, and a half hour for you."

Fabrizio laughed. It felt so good to laugh. "That is true!" He looked at the boys' faces. "That is because I was not lucky enough to be in Brother Emilian's classes when I was a boy."

The students grinned and looked proud.

"Emilian is also an excellent barber. See this?" Fabrizio bent down so the boys could see the rounded top of his shaved, tonsured head. "No cuts! Smooth as a pebble. We used to have Brother Silvanus here as barber. He didn't realize he couldn't see very well. When he finished, my head had as many lines in it as that rope you have in your hands."

The boys groaned in glee at the thought of this. One covered his head with his hands in mock defense.

Fabrizio laughed again. "I don't want to interrupt your important work any longer," he said. He nodded to Emilian. "Thank you, my friend. Most sincerely."

"You are welcome." Emilian lifted his rope in the air. "All right now, hold it straight like this," he called out.

Eight pairs of hands went to work again.

FABRIZIO TURNED BACK toward his patient herd and the momentary lightness vanished. Nobilus was standing in the middle of the goats. Manus stood in front of the library doors watching. The two looked as if they had been talking together just moments before.

"Good day, Fabrizio," Nobilus said, as he held out his hands to the curious muzzles. "How were the goats this morning?"

Fabrizio was surprised at being so addressed, and cautious. But he had to give Nobilus the respect and consideration that were due a guest, a guest far superior to himself. "They are well, producing much milk," he said, "and I like to think they are happy."

Nobilus bent and stroked the goat nearest him. It was Sancha, and Sancha closed her eyes in enjoyment. Lily stayed back, on guard as usual.

"I must say," Nobilus said, "the cheese they produce is excellent. I have not had goat cheese in many years and I enjoy your Friar's Cheese very much."

Fabrizio felt bewildered at this. He expected complaint,

not praise. "Thank you, sir. Gustave makes it. I help him sometimes, but the flavors he uses are his secret alone."

"My father was a Genoese," said Nobilus. "But my mother was French. She disdained goat cheese and would have nothing in our house except the cheese from cows or sheep. I tasted goat cheese for the first time when I visited my father's relatives and loved it." He gave Sancha a final pat and pointed at Ermentrude.

"This one does not have horns?"

"It happens occasionally in that breed. It would explain why she was given to us."

Nobilus nodded and began to turn away, his mind seemingly already elsewhere. "Give Gustave my compliments."

Fabrizio gave a little bow. "I will."

He called to the goats and they moved again toward the stables, though he looked back over his shoulder at the Dominican. Nobilus had almost rejoined Manus. But the expression on Manus's face had not changed. It was sober and watchful and wary, just as it had been when Fabrizio had been introduced to him the day the Dominicans arrived.

A thought struck him as he went through the pen door with the goats. The force of it made him stumble into Ermentrude who bleated her surprise. Could it be that Manus wasn't here to watch just the Spirituals? Was he here to watch them as well?

HE MADE the goats comfortable in their pen, pulling a little hay down and filling their water trough. When he crossed the courtyard again, Manus and Nobilus had already gone. He shook his head at his fears and headed toward the kitchen to help Gustave with the meal.

Leo had twisted his ankle badly last night and would not be here to help today. His grandfather had brought a donkey so the boy could ride back to his home. And for some reason, Donatello needed this day to give the numbers boy an accounting lesson.

As he was thinking of these things, and walking toward the side of the kitchen, the kitchen door opened and Gustave came out, hurrying to meet him.

"The Spirituals are in there," he said, half in a whisper.

"In where?" asked Fabrizio.

"In the kitchen. What do I do?"

"What are they doing?"

Gustave rubbed the palm of his hand roughly on the side of his bald head. "They want to help," he said. "And I don't know what to do. They are prisoners. The pope is angry at them. I don't know if I should allow them in the kitchen."

"I will come, Gustave."

Fabrizio entered the kitchen, Gustave right behind him. Three of the Spirituals stood awkwardly by the large wooden work table and Fabrizio was relieved to see that Venedictos and Sereno were not among them.

"My name is Fabrizio," he said. "What are your names?"

The older one with the short hooked nose and gray in his hair answered. "I am Lucien. This is Palmer, and our youngest there is Honorato."

Honorato. The hungry-looking boy whom he had taken cheese to that first night. All three looked cautious, and the air of defeat seemed to rest upon them.

"We have come to help in the kitchen," Lucien went on.

"Please give us the humblest of tasks, for that is what we wish."

The humblest tasks were, of course, what Saint Francis had urged on his followers dozens of years ago. Fabrizio glanced at Gustave, but the cook didn't open his mouth. He stood, more nervous than Fabrizio had ever seen him, waiting for Fabrizio to solve this problem.

Fabrizio cleared his throat. "I don't know how to distinguish which are the humblest tasks of the kitchen. We all tend to do whatever needs to be done when it comes time to do it. To be the greatest help, you would need to do whatever Gustave asks whenever he tells you, whether that means taking serving trays into the dining hall or scrubbing the kitchen floor."

"We will do that," said Lucien.

"Good, thank you." Fabrizio turned to Gustave. "What should we do first?"

Gustave bent his head toward Fabrizio's and whispered. "Will you stay here as long as they are here?"

"Yes," said Fabrizio, smiling to reassure the cook.

Gustave was still hesitant to speak to the rebellious friars. "Our silent boy couldn't come today either. His mother had a baby yesterday and wants him home."

"Well, then, it is good we have help." Fabrizio tried to speak confidently, anything to stir the life in his friend. "What must be done? Pour the beer? Get the loaves ready to take in? Did the young shoemakers already come get their eggs to take home?"

Gustave nodded but still did not move.

Fabrizio glanced around. "Here, the barrel has been

brought up from the cellar." He motioned to Lucien. "If you would start over here? The cups are on the shelf there."

A strange look came over Lucien's face.

Fabrizio hesitated. What had he said that was not right? *The cellar.* That was it. He remembered talk of a controversy over friaries storing grain or drink in their cellars. Poor friars didn't do such things. True Franciscans wouldn't do such things.

He felt the urge to take Lucien down to the cellar to show him the large empty room, and three lonely barrels that sat at the foot of the stairs. The friary was usually only days away from thirst. A new barrel or money for one was usually given just in time, which made Donatello very anxious, but bothered the friars barely at all.

Should he tell Lucien this? Would Lucien believe his explanation any more than Sereno had? If he could believe it, wouldn't he still find fault?

Fabrizio pretended he had not seen the look. He took a cup down and showed Lucien how to tap the barrel to fill it.

"Just set it here on the table and the server will put them on a tray and take it in."

"I can serve too," said Lucien.

"Good." Fabrizio pointed at another shelf. "The trays are kept there. No more than six cups at a time on a tray. Gustave is very particular about that."

Lucien nodded. "I will be careful."

Fabrizio turned back around. "Now, Gustave? Where is the broad bowl that Honorato here can serve the bread loaves in?"

The cook finally moved into action. "Here," he said

gruffly, handing Honorato the large bowl. "The eggs are boiled and waiting too."

"I can serve the eggs," said Palmer.

Gustave nodded. "The cheese, Fabrizio. We must use up the last of that round before we start this one."

Fabrizio cut soft chunks of the cheese and piled it on the accustomed cheese board. As he worked he could hear the hall fill with people. Subdued voices. The scraping of benches on the stone floor. Respectful greetings as the Guardian entered. The heavy tread of the Dominicans' boots. The expectant, waiting hush.

"Is everything filled?" Fabrizio looked around the kitchen. All eyes were nervous and all were upon him.

"Follow me into the hall," he said. "We will stand along the wall and wait in a row, just as you have seen every day, and our Guardian will ask a blessing on the food."

They quietly followed him in and obediently lined up along the wall. Fabrizio with the cheese board, Lucien with a tray of beer, Palmer with the eggs, and lastly Honorato holding a bowl of bread twice as wide as he was. After one furtive glance through the doorway, Gustave stayed in the kitchen.

Fabrizio turned his head toward the Guardian, his gaze sweeping the room. Many of the faces were staring at him with odd expressions. Cantor wore his wry and curious look, one eyebrow raised in a questioning arch. Emilian looked irritated; Kerstan puzzled. Manus and Nobilus narrowed suspicious eyes; gone was the former friendliness over the goats. Against his will, Fabrizio checked the back table. The lines on Venedictos' face were almost mocking. Sereno was unreadable.

They all bowed their heads as the Guardian began to pray. Fabrizio's mind whirled as he struggled to understand. What had come over the dining hall? Why would they look at him so?

Suddenly, he grasped what they had seen.

He, Fabrizio, was with the Spirituals. Standing alongside them. Looking like one of them.

12

His heart pounded as he took the cheese board up and down the rows. He kept his head down so he would not have to meet anyone's eyes. No one spoke to him as he served them, except the scriveners who seemed oblivious to the tension in the room. No customary nods of gratitude from his brothers. His stomach twisted inside of him.

He had just finished with the Dominican table when he heard Nobilus speak in a low voice. "The poison spreads, Titus. You see? Isn't this proof of it?" Fabrizio did not linger to hear the answer.

When he went to sit down on the bench at the end of his usual table, Emilian slid a few inches away from him. Fabrizio's thoughts spun in confusion. What did they think of him? Why? How could he have done anything different? Was it wrong to show the Spirituals how to serve the food? A small pain ignited in his stomach, burning low, but insistent.

The Guardian was turning pages, preparing to read to the

company while they ate. Fabrizio bent across the table toward Cantor and whispered. "They came to the kitchen this morning. Gustave didn't know what to do with them." He hoped Emilian had heard. That he would not judge him falsely.

Cantor nodded. "The infirmary too," he said quietly. "Quintus said—"

The Guardian's voice broke through. "Today, for our meditations, we will begin Saint Paul's letter to the Romans. Since the visiting scholars are hard at work on copies of this holy book, it is fitting that we read it together also as a community." The Guardian smiled at them all and began to read.

"*Paul, a servant of Christ Jesus, called to be an apostle and set apart for the gospel of God...*"

The room was silent except for the quiet meeting of wood on wood as cups of beer were supped and returned to the table. There was the occasional cough, the slight crackle of tearing bread, the light shatter of eggshell, and the sound of the Guardian's voice. Everything that used to be peaceful.

"*...who through the Spirit of holiness was declared with power to be the Son of God by his resurrection from the dead...*"

Inside Fabrizio's head was a roaring rush of feeling. Since the first day the Spirituals had come, it had been hard to sit and listen to the reading of Scripture with them in the same room. It was especially hard now.

"*...And you also are among those who are called to belong to Jesus Christ. To all in Rome who are loved by God and called to be saints....*"

Ever since they had come, the Spirituals had destroyed the harmony and peace of this place. Made the San Stigliano friars defensive. Brought the inquisitors down upon them.

And now, to have anyone think for the slightest moment that he—that he...

He bent low to his plate and pressed his fingers hard into the corners of his eyes. *That he would join those who condemn their Franciscan life? That he would reject his own brothers like that?* He could not bear it. The flame in his stomach grew and he could not eat.

The Guardian read on, his voice calm and steady. "*I long to see you so that I may impart to you some spiritual gift to make you strong—that is, that you and I may be mutually encouraged by each other's faith. I do not want you to be unaware, brothers...*"

The ache in Fabrizio's stomach burned alarmingly. He knew from experience that if he did not see Quintus soon, he would be faint. He stood slowly and walked toward the kitchen door. The Guardian stopped speaking, and once again there was a horrible moment of everyone's eyes on him.

"Fabrizio?" said the Guardian. "What is it, my son?"

There. The Guardian had called him "son." The name he had called him ever since he first saw the boy Fabrizio huddled outside the friary gates so many years ago. And he had called him this in front of them all. Fabrizio took heart.

"I—I am not well. I will go to the infirmary by your permission."

The Guardian dipped his head. "Go in peace."

Fabrizio bowed his thanks and left through the kitchen door. He did not delay to speak with Gustave. Had no time to answer the surprised look on the cook's face. The pain in his stomach sharpened. Beads of sweat broke out on his forehead.

He went through the kitchen, one hand pressed against

his belly, and out the door, alongside the gardens to the infirmary.

Quintus got up from his chair the moment he saw him. "Is it bad again, Fabrizio? Like it was the summer you returned from Milan?"

That was the summer Fabrizio had been a postulant. The summer he had completed his training and taken his vows. He had been so afraid the *Custode* would send him far away from San Stigliano. And the fear had burned his stomach. None of the physicians in Milan helped him. Only Quintus. Only coming home.

"Yes, a bit like that," he said weakly.

Quintus took his arm. "Here, lie down."

Fabrizio laid down on the cot Quintus led him to. It was along a wall and Fabrizio turned toward the whitewashed stone, wanting to hide his face from anyone that might come through the door.

He was shaking when Quintus covered him with a blanket, but he knew it was not with fever. The blanket was a welcome covering, a place in which to hide his fears.

He closed his eyes and heard sounds of pouring and stirring, the gentle clink of the pottery dishes, the marble mortar and pestle grinding together, and the rumbling hum that meant Quintus was thinking.

"Here you are, Fabrizio." Quintus bent over him. "Sit up and let's get a spoonful of this elecampene and honey in you first. Good. Now some bites of bay laurel cake. No, you can't lie back down yet. One more thing. You must have several swallows of this wine. It contains butcher's broom. All right. Now you rest. When you wake up, I'll have hot peppermint water for you."

He ate and drank obediently, then turned gratefully toward the wall and closed his eyes again. The older man's hand rested lightly on his head. Gentle words filled his ears. A prayer to the Healer of all. A prayer for Fabrizio.

HE FINALLY FELL asleep in the white cheerful room with polished wood floors, a crackling fire on the hearth, and Quintus working with dried leaves and ground powders at his table, humming all the while. Fabrizio slept on until the scraping of a stool and the presence of another person nearby awoke him. He blinked and turned on his cot to see the Guardian sitting by his side, looking at him with compassion in his eyes.

"Your color has come back." The Guardian rested a gentle hand on Fabrizio's head. "How are you feeling, my son?"

"I do not know," he whispered. "My stomach is better, but my mind—my mind is blurred."

The Guardian, too, prayed for him, while Fabrizio closed his eyes and listened.

When the words ceased, Fabrizio stared up at the wooden slats on the ceiling and spoke the first words that came to his mind, even as he wondered if they were the right ones.

"This community, these brothers, mean so much to me." His voice broke.

"It is good that they do, my son." The Guardian spoke reassuringly. "Very good. But you must always ask yourself, does Christ mean even more to me?"

The question sounded odd to him, thrust as it was into his confusion. "Of course He would, wouldn't He? " said

Fabrizio, "If there is love for my brothers?" He saw their faces in his mind—generous Gustave, the talented Emilian, clever Cantor, patient Kerstan, wise Quintus, the unexcitable Benefice. And Donatello too.

"There is truth in that, yes," said the Guardian. "But it rests in the arms of a greater truth. That is, when we love Christ first and above all, then we love our brothers best."

Fabrizio kept his gaze on the ceiling, repeating the words over and over in his mind.

"Have I done wrong, my Guardian?" he asked, fearing the answer.

The Guardian patted his arm. "Only as we all have, Fabrizio. Our brothers are easily seen, while Christ our true Lord now is invisible. I do not know exactly what ails you, but I do know this: When you walk hand in hand with Christ, aware every moment of the love and power of His great sacrifice for you, that heals many things."

Fabrizio's bewilderment increased. Was the Guardian now concerned about his faith? Was it because he had associated with the Spirituals? He felt his face grow warm.

"But I am a Christian," he protested. "I have been a Christian for years. I *know* this."

The Guardian nodded his head in agreement. "Even so, yes, Fabrizio. It is just as you say. We know this, and yet—and yet—it is so great we can barely know it. I feel the greatness of it every day. So every day I strive and pray to know it more."

He rose from the stool. "Stay here and rest, Fabrizio. I will take your session of prayers for the people. Eat and drink whatever Quintus feels you should. Then see if you are ready to be with your goats this evening. I will ask Emilian to draw water for them, and Gustave can send Benefice to the pen with scraps. Meanwhile, pray over what I have told you and watch for Christ. Always think, where is Christ? Look for him, walk with Him, and let your mind be filled with His great love for you."

"Thank you, my Guardian," Fabrizio whispered, his eyes on the ceiling.

The older man leaned over the cot and made the sign of the cross above Fabrizio's head. "God's peace, Fabrizio."

13

———

He stayed in the infirmary until Compline, having broth and bread for his dinner, dutifully swallowing all the herbal brews Quintus urged upon him. When the night bell rang, he and the old healer knelt by the fireplace and chanted their prayers together.

Quintus patted his shoulder. "A good night's sleep and you should feel well enough in the morning. Ah," he added, shaking his head, "it is not pleasant to have a troublesome stomach!"

In the stable, the goats crowded around him, shoving insistent noses into his hands, begging for a scratch. Ermentrude bleated like a worried mother. He begged their pardon for the late milking, then sang to them a quiet psalm of grace and mercy while he filled the pails.

Gustave put the milk in a pot over the fire. He shook off Fabrizio's regret over the late hour with a smile. "I knew it would be coming, so I finished everything else first. It is all right. Go sleep, Fabrizio."

He climbed the stairs slowly, glad that the stairway and halls were already dark and quiet. Glad that his bed waited for him. Glad too that Emilian and Kerstan were already sleeping.

In the morning, a loud commotion in the stables next door made Fabrizio step outside during the early milking to see what was happening. The Dominican servants scurried around, pulling the coaches from the stables, harnessing horses, and loading bags and packs. Kerstan came over to stand by Fabrizio as they watched.

"They are going to Avignon to meet with the pope," Kerstan said. "Cardinal Scantoni is there too, waiting for them. It will take almost a week to get to Avignon, so they will be gone for some time." He shook his head thoughtfully. "I wonder what they will tell the pope, and, also, what the pope will tell them."

"The talks are still not going well?" Fabrizio asked.

Kerstan shook his head. "I could not imagine them going so badly."

Fabrizio looked closely at him as he spoke. Kerstan's manner was what it always had been, that of older brother, tutor, and friend. The judgment that Fabrizio had felt from his brothers yesterday, had that been real? Was it fear, instead, that made Fabrizio think his brothers looked down on him? Fear that made him see lies? Relieved, he took a deep breath.

"And what about the copying of Romans for the Visconti?"

Kerstan sighed. "It's going very slow, but we will have more time now. I hope to finish it by the time the Dominicans return."

EVEN THOUGH THE Spirituals were bound to stay at San Stigliano, the departure of the inquisitors removed at least one of the dark clouds hanging over the friary. The Spirituals still sat on their separate bench in the chapel during the chanting of the Divine Office, and still slept in their rooms at the far end of the dormitory, but they were more active in the friary—mopping, sweeping, scrubbing, cleaning.

Lucien plucked chickens with Gustave and filled the roasting pan with gifts of sausage the farmers brought in. Lucien's parents had owned a small inn, and he had grown up in the kitchen. With Lucien helping him, Gustave did not overcook the sausage and it no longer burst its skins. The scriveners and the *poverelli* were loud in their approval.

Lucien and Palmer continued to serve at table and also helped the group of lay brothers who worked in the laundry. Another Spiritual—Laudalino—helped Quintus in the infirmary, attending to the friary's needs while Quintus and Cantor tended the sick in town. The additional help was welcomed when two of the scriveners burned themselves trying to move a boiling ink pot, and when Prentice sliced his hand sharpening his pen.

Sereno did not come to see Fabrizio in the goat pens again, and Fabrizio was glad of that. His heart was too pained by the separation between them to risk another talk. No one in the friary knew that Sereno, now so disapproving, had once been Fabrizio's friend. That hurt he carried deep in himself alone.

Once, as Fabrizio and the goats came in the friary gate, he saw Sereno scrubbing the library steps on his hands and knees. Sereno may have smiled at him or frowned, Fabrizio could not tell, the sunshine creating shadows as it did. He returned an uncertain smile and led the goats to their pen.

Somehow it was easier to talk to Honorato, the youngest poor one. Fabrizio showed him how to milk the goats and offered to take him to the hills with the herd. But Venedictos did not want Honorato to go at first. Was he afraid that Fabrizio would discuss the vows of poverty with the young man? Seek to persuade him to leave his fellows and become a convent friar? Then, suddenly, without explanation, Venedictos changed his mind and Honorato came to the goat pen with permission to go.

The youngest Spiritual made a pleasant, but quiet companion. They set out, walking on either side of the goats, with Ermentrude in the lead and Lily, watchful, as the last. They waved at the scriveners who were combing the hillside oaks to find more gall nuts for their ink. Fabrizio introduced Honorato to Old Leonard and his sons as they passed by. The peasant pulled some bread from his bag and insisted on giving it to them.

At noontime, they ate their meal in friendly, though cautious, silence, sharing a fallen log as a bench, while the goats foraged among the brush. But when the distant sound of the chapel bell rang out, Honorato stepped away toward a rocky outcropping and said his prayers by himself.

Fabrizio felt a stab of pain. *Why could they not pray together?*

He knelt in the grass and put one arm around Ermentrude's neck instead, and there he prayed his psalms. Afterwards, they brought the goats down from the hills in silence. Even though it was too soon for the Dominicans to return, Fabrizio was still afraid that somehow they would have come in their absence and be angry that he had taken Honorato outside the gates.

Fabrizio paid closer attention to the Divine Office than ever before. He listened carefully at each reading of Scripture for every mention of Christ. The Spirituals confused him. Hurt him. And he needed to know what God thought. The Guardian was right. It was good—necessary—to always watch for Christ.

Daily he reviewed the one hundred verses he had memorized, and he prayed often in the goat pen. After one such session, he rose from his knees to find Honorato in the doorway watching him, forehead puckered, confusion in his eyes.

"You pray to God as if He were your uncle," he said.

Fabrizio did not know if this was meant to be criticism. Embarrassed, he shook the straw from his robe. "I would not know. I have never had an uncle."

"That is the way I used to talk to mine."

"He must be a good uncle, then." He pointed to a hook on the wall of the pen. "Get the pitchfork. It is time to get more hay for the goats."

KERSTAN AND PRENTICE were the happiest people in the friary. Now, at last, the copying of the book of Romans proceeded according to plan. On his rest breaks under the tree in their courtyard, Prentice unwrapped his bandaged hand to show Fabrizio how it was healing.

"There is no infection," said Fabrizio, examining the clean line.

"None at all," said Prentice, wrapping the thin strips of bandage around his hand again. "You friars are the best healers."

"Quintus knows more about herbs than I can imagine."

"I'm sure he does, but this was the new friar. The one with the long name that begins with an 'L'."

Oh. "Laudalino?"

"Yes."

Fabrizio would rather the praise had gone to Quintus. He changed the subject. "And how far are you now in the copy?"

"The twelfth chapter." There was glee in the scrivener's voice. And pride. He looked up to the branches of the tree and recited. "*...in Christ we who are many form one body, and each member belongs to all the others.*"

"Very nice. That is one of the verses I say every day." He did not say that it had been one of his favorites. At least before this time of confusion had come. Now it only made him uneasy. It spoke of a unity, of a belonging together, that he no longer felt. It was hard to think of such Scriptures while seeing the opposite of them every day.

Prentice leaned back against the tree again, his thoughts taking him to a far different place.

"I think the Visconti will be pleased," he said. "Once they see my work...well, this could be the start of a great life for me." He sighed, a huge grin on his face, his gaze aimed past the open gates of San Stigliano to the broad land beyond, where with a pen and ink he could write an amazing future for himself.

THE DOMINICANS RETURNED on a day in early October, arriving before Vespers. A chill rain fell, making the ground sodden, caking their coach wheels and horses' hooves with mud. They had brought even more servants with them, servants who efficiently moved the horses and coaches into the stable and unloaded them, shouting all the while in rapid French.

Nobilus had a determined set to his walk, a new confidence in his posture, as when a hard and disagreeable problem has been solved. Titus wore a continually troubled look on his face. Manus remained unchanged.

Gustave worried about there being food enough. He tore up the few roasted chickens and threw smaller and smaller pieces into the soup with the squash to make the soup in the guest pot go farther. He sent Benefice and Palmer scurrying to the garden to hoist another row of beans from the soil, then hung the withered tawny pods upside down over the fire, fretting that the rain had made them not dry enough to cook. Fabrizio fetched cheese from the storeroom, and noticed the many bare shelves.

In the end, Donatello sent to his house in town for provisions. "Just for the present crisis," he told the Guardian.

That night at dinner, Lucien and Palmer began to serve the tables as they had often done. At the Dominican table, there came a sharp command which drew everyone's attention.

Nobilus held up his hands as if to ward off evil. "I will not take my soup from your disobedient hands, nor any food either. Get away from us."

A scared silence fell on the room. Palmer backed away, his face reddening, white fingers gripping the tray.

Cantor stood up. "Come, Fabrizio," he whispered.

The two of them took the dishes and trays from Lucien and Palmer. Fabrizio tried to send Palmer an expression of sympathy, but the young man would not look at him. Cantor offered the soup to Nobilus again and the inquisitor took the bowl with a satisfied smile.

When the whole dining hall had been served, they sat down to an eerily quiet dinner amongst their fellows. The *poverelli* drew closer to each other at their table by the fire, newly afraid of these robed, religious men that filled the room.

The friars themselves remained silent, listening instead to the slurp and slosh of soup into dozens of mouths, the crack of the logs in the fireplace, the rain against the windows, the hushed conversation from the scriveners' table, and Nobilus telling the Guardian of the deplorable state of the roads.

Fabrizio stole glances at the Spirituals' table. They appeared to eat calmly. Sereno's back was to him, as were Laudalino's and Palmer's. But Venedictos, Lucien, and Honorato faced the room with resolute looks on their faces.

14

The cold rain continued throughout the night and pattered steadily on the roof of the goat pen the next morning. Fabrizio was hastening to bring the first milk to Gustave, when Emilian came across the square to meet him, his hood pulled over his head against the damp.

"The Spirituals will not be eating with us today," he said.

Fabrizio hunched over his pail to protect it from the rain. He felt a flash of alarm at Emilian's words.

"Why? Are they not to eat at all?"

Emilian shook his head. "They have been ordered to stay in their rooms for three days of fasting and prayer. After that they will speak with the inquisitors again." He kept pace with Fabrizio as they moved toward the kitchen. "Maybe then they will come to their senses and stop making trouble for us."

"Maybe," said Fabrizio. With Emilian close behind, he ducked into the kitchen door. But as he poured the milk into Gustave's waiting kettle, he remembered Sereno's life-long quest for peace. Would three days of prayer change what Sereno considered the answer to twenty years of prayer?

As he went about his daily tasks, making his way around the puddles that filled the courtyard, Fabrizio could not help but glance up at the windows of the rooms assigned to the Spirituals. There, behind the leaded glass, there the poor ones prayed.

A sense of desolation welled up in him, a sense he did not understand. He pushed the feeling from his thoughts, pulled his hood more tightly around his head, and went on his way before his stomach could trouble him again.

THE CALM that usually accompanied days of fasting and prayer was dashed by the formidable presence of the Dominicans. They and their companions filled three benches in the chapel. Their chanting drowned out all the Franciscan voices, even Cantor's marvelously clear tenor.

The inquisitor's group seemed to be everywhere Fabrizio turned—in the stables, the library, the hallway outside the chapel prayer rooms, the kitchen, the infirmary, the cheese storeroom. And even once in the goat pen, where their sudden appearing made Lily unable to let down her milk.

Everything they saw, they examined with searching eyes. Everywhere they went resounded with their voices. Bold, laughing, arguing voices, speaking mostly French, which Fabrizio did not understand. Whatever they requested, the friars did. It was as if the lord of the old manor had resurrected and returned, making all the friars his servants.

Fabrizio tried to stay out of their way. He spent his time

praying for the town folk, taking his turns cleaning and serving, helping Gustave stretch the food in the kitchen, waiting at table, and tending his goats. And the last was a greater concern. He had to make sure that Ermentrude and the others ate well, because in a month they would be mated.

A farmer south of town, a friend of Old Leonard's, would come with his ox-pulled wagon and take the herd to his large goat pens where his hardy males would do the job. Fabrizio's goats would be returned and when the does gave birth in the spring, milk production would increase. At the right time, each baby goat would be given to a poor family.

He sat on the stool in the middle of the pen thinking of all these things, when Ermentrude rested her head on his knee. He smiled and rubbed her neck and hornless head firmly, lovingly. Her little friend Sancha pushed toward him for her share of the affection, shoving her nose into the palm of his hand, her horns pointed carefully away.

Fabrizio's heart warmed within him. He loved caring for the goats. They were the animals that had taken to him when he was a despairing child. He had found healing in tending these creatures; he needed their healing presence now.

He wanted to pray, but the words would not form in his mind, even the words he had memorized and spoken so many times. In truth, he was afraid a Dominican would overhear him and disapprove of something. He turned instead to the portions of Scripture that the Guardian had selected for each member of this Franciscan community to learn and keep close to his heart.

"This is from Exodus, Sancha," he said, keeping his voice low. "*In your unfailing love you will lead the people you have redeemed. In your strength you will guide them to your holy dwelling.* That was after the Israelites crossed the Red Sea," he said rubbing behind her ears.

"And this one for you, Ermentrude, from Romans. *But God demonstrates his own love for us in this: While we were still sinners, Christ died for us.*

"There it is, my sisters, redemption in the Old Testament and redemption in the New! Our Lord does not change."

Ermentrude made her deep, throaty, contented sound and Fabrizio smiled to himself. What an easy congregation he had to tend! One that matched his talents, surely.

He stood in awe of the preaching ability that the Guardian and Kerstan displayed Sunday after Sunday in the friary chapel, and on special occasions at the church in Armonia. In words so full of humanity, and so full of Scripture, they made Christ seen. And, oh, how their hearers rejoiced!

"Because, of course, where you see Christ, there you see God," he said out loud, scratching underneath Ermentrude's chin. The Guardian was right in telling him to always look for Christ.

Fabrizio smiled at his four-legged parishioners. "And where is Christ in your passage, Sancha? He is leading his people whom He has redeemed with His unfailing love. Now, in Leviticus we come to loving our neighbor--"

A figure appeared in the doorway. But it was not Sereno. Of course not. He would be in his room praying. Fasting. Hungry. Instead Kerstan walked in, a frown on his face.

"You don't have a fire here, but at least it's warm enough."

Fabrizio rose and nudged the stool toward his friend. "What brings you here?"

"Confession," Kerstan replied, settling his tall frame onto the short stool. "I am weary of people."

Fabrizio smiled. "Goats make good company. Their arguments are fixed more easily, for they all want the same things in the end."

Kerstan appeared too distracted to attend to this, so Fabrizio picked up a comb Old Leonard had given him and began working through the tangles in Ermentrude's long, gray coat. He waited a few moments before offering his second question.

"How is the copy coming?"

Kerstan gave a frustrated laugh. "It should be going well, since the debates have not started again, but it is not. Nobilus and some of the others insist on watching, and because of that the scriveners are making many mistakes. Even Prentice. Sometimes especially Prentice. If caught quickly, errors can be picked out. Others the illustrator will be able to cover. But this is not like him." He took up a piece of straw, just like Sereno had done, and twisted it in his hands.

Fabrizio waved the comb in the air with his question. "Why do they watch so closely?"

Kerstan rolled his eyes. "Who could know? They may have particular reasons, some hidden orders from either the pope or Cardinal Scantoni. But I think when a person is given the task of looking for error, he finds it easy to be consumed with that task and to never stop watching."

"And it makes all those who are watched," said Fabrizio, "afraid of a guilt they do not have."

Kerstan raised his head to look at him. "That is exactly it." He sighed, tossed the bit of straw to the ground, and picked up another one before speaking again. This time in a lower voice.

"The Guardian is under a great strain. He does not say it, does not speak ill of anyone, but I can tell he does not like the presence of the Dominicans."

"The Dominicans would not need to be here if it were not for the stubbornness of the Spirituals," said Fabrizio. His comb paused halfway down Ermentrude's side. *Did he really feel that way?* Still?

Kerstan did not notice Fabrizio's internal struggle. "True," he replied, "but Cardinal Scantoni should have picked a different place for this fruitless debate, so our work would not be interfered with. The copying is going too slowly.

"We have had several letters from Milan asking about it. I have explained the reason for the delay, and they do not like that either. Maybe I should not have done that. The Visconti are not good friends with the Cardinal, and for that reason he stays in Genoa instead of Milan."

Kerstan shrugged his shoulders. "They have their struggles, we have ours. Because of our guests, the Guardian cannot leave to go to his work in town. Even the *Custode* has told him to stay close. Also, the Guardian has told Donatello not to start on the chapel roof until this is resolved. So the wood just sits and waits when carpenters in town would benefit from having the work to do."

"And the buckets in the chapel keep filling?"

"And the buckets in the chapel keep filling." Kerstan tossed his straw to the ground again and rubbed his hands together. "Winter will be here before two months are out. Ice on the roof will make the holes worse."

"Does the Guardian believe this *will* be resolved? That all will end well?"

"He has not spoken of it to me. There is a chance, I suppose, that Cardinal Scantoni might change his mind."

Fabrizio plied the comb again. "The cardinal does not sound like a man who would back down. Neither does the pope."

"No, definitely not. I was only hoping. It is more likely that the Spirituals would be forced to live out their days among us. As prisoners."

The thought of living the rest of his life underneath those hostile, accusing looks made Fabrizio's stomach sink. He plucked at a pine needle that had embedded itself in Ermentrude's coat. Sereno would never be content here. But then, no one was content here now.

Another thought pursued that one. "Venedictos would never submit to our Guardian's rule."

Kerstan gave a wry laugh. "No. Never." He looked up at Fabrizio. "The Guardian is grateful to you for showing kindness to our en—, I mean, to the rigorists."

Fabrizio's arm held still. "What do you mean?"

"You showed Lucien, Palmer, and Honorato how to serve and help Gustave. That was the first step for all of us. You made it easier for the rest of us to work with them."

The last of his former fear shriveled and blew away. Serving with the Spirituals had not divided him from his brothers after all. He pulled the pine needle out of Ermentrude's hair and picked up the comb again. Relief surged through him even as he replied to what Kerstan had been saying. "What does it mean now? The Dominicans will not let the poor ones help any more."

Kerstan got to his feet and shook the straw from his robe. "Yes. That is bad. Quintus already misses Laudalino's help in the infirmary. There is fever in the town to attend to, and one of the Dominican horses stepped on a groom's foot. The foot is black in places and swollen. But Quintus and Cantor cannot be both places. It's a shame the man won't let a Spiritual touch him."

Before Kerstan could leave, Fabrizio reached out his hand to make him pause so he could ask one more question. "Today is the third day of fasting and prayer. Tomorrow the Dominicans and the Spirituals meet again?"

Kerstan nodded with a rueful smile. "I have my pencils and paper all ready. I will be sitting in the gallery, writing down every word."

When Fabrizio awoke the next morning, his first thought was that today the Spirituals would be able to eat again. The thought filled him with relief, and he didn't think to question it. Instead, he pulled on his robe and hurried through the early morning chill to the goat pen. No clouds blocked the sky, and the morning stars glittered freely.

As usual, the goats had less milk to give as autumn deepened, so the milking did not take him long. He was glad when the task was finished and he could enter the much warmer kitchen where Gustave and Leo, still favoring his hurt ankle, were taking loaves from the oven.

"Good morning and God's peace to you," he said, as he poured the milk into the large kettle. He set down the bucket by the sink and opened his cloth sack, holding it out towards the cook.

"So you are going to the hills today, Fabrizio?" Gustave

asked, as he used his wooden paddle to slide a warm loaf into the sack.

"I will go every day I can before the winter comes. Winter is a long, unhappy time for a goat."

"And a man," said Gustave. Before he could say more, a loud clatter sounded behind him. Leo had backed the handles of his wooden paddle into the fire irons.

Fabrizio quickly reached for the fallen irons and hung them on their hooks over the hearth. "All is well, Leo, all is well. How is your ankle today? Still sore?"

Leo nodded sheepishly.

"Healing can be a tiresomely long thing," Fabrizio said, giving the boy a quick pat on the shoulder.

Gustave added some boiled eggs to the sack. "The loaves are so hot, I think the cheese would melt. Eggs might be best."

"That's just fine, Gustave. Thank you."

He did not bother to take any beer or ale with him. He had his wooden cup, and on the mountain the springs of water were fresh and unpolluted.

HE OPENED THE PEN DOOR, called the goats to him, and picked up his walking staff. They crossed the quiet square to the small door by the unopened gate. He took the key from its peg on the stone wall and thrust it into the iron lock. Returning the key, he ushered his goats through the opening and out to their freedom. Yet, he could not help but look back across the square toward the dormitory. Toward the row of darkened windows where the Spirituals slept.

Pain stabbed Fabrizio's heart. How could it be that he and his only childhood friend had followed their dreams to join the same holy order, only to end up as enemies? It shouldn't be that way. Instead of arguing and accusation, shouldn't it be the love of God that flowed between them? Then there would be healing, or as Kerstan once put it, the mending of souls.

He looked again at those stubborn, silent windows and a surge of frustration filled him. Anger followed quickly after. He shut the door in the wall firmly.

"Ermentrude! Lily! Get your sisters. Let's go!"

The goats moved toward the familiar path, but Ermentrude butted his leg as she passed. There had been no reason for the sharp tone in his voice, and she knew it.

THE GOATS SEEMED POSSESSED with a mischievous spirit that day. They butted and kicked each other, and even ran from him, ignoring his calls. In their petulant moods they scattered far across the hillside, something they had never done. A few of them moved far up the hill into the pine trees and out of sight.

"Stop!" he cried. "What has come over you? Has the friary infected you? Sancha, Ermentrude! Where are you?"

Fierce growls sounded behind him, and in an instant, two large brown dogs with matted coats and large, terrible jaws shot past him and into the trees after the goats.

Fabrizio let out a cry and chased after them. One turned on him and Fabrizio struck it hard with his staff. It howled and spun around, then shook itself, and raced toward the goats again.

The flock ran wildly, scattering in every direction. They turned to use their horns against the dogs, then forgot in their panic. The trees dwindled and their flight brought them out in the open again. Some goats leapt toward the safety of the rocky outcroppings.

Fabrizio screamed as he ran among them, trying to distract the dogs, to pull them away from their prey. He got close enough again to swing the staff solidly against a dog's shoulder. Once against a back. They were so fast that the staff missed often, but at last a solid blow made one of them turn away.

He stood guard, catching his breath, watching as it ran, until it disappeared into the smoke of another peasant's burning field.

He turned and studied the hillside keenly for the other dog. No growling came to his ears. No sounds of frenzied flight. The chase had led them back to familiar ground, a foraging area not far from where Old Leonard pastured his sheep.

He took a deep breath and wiped his brow with the sleeve of his robe. "Ermentrude! Sancha! Lily!" he called. "Gather your sisters!"

The goats returned to him, bleating and wailing, needing comfort. He caressed them with shaking hands. One had a torn and bloody flank. Sancha had scratches from the chase. But they had survived, able to outrun and out leap the dogs.

He kept calling for the stragglers, slowly leading them to the familiar boulder and the well-loved place in the sun. Suddenly, over them all, the cry of a single goat pierced the hills, a haunting, tragic cry. Fabrizio hurried toward the sound. He rounded a thicket of trees and saw the other dog.

The shaggy brown beast was lying on its side in the scrub grass of the hillside. Lily stood next to him, shrieking with all her might. Blood smeared her horns and her sleek brown coat. But she was standing.

"Lily! Lily!" he called, running forward, wielding his staff again. But there was no need.

The dog did not move. His neck had been pierced. The blood on Lily's horns was not her own.

Yet, Lily would not let him come near to comfort her. Instead she moved back and pushed through the clumps of tall grass. He followed her, speaking gently, trying to calm her, but she would not stop wailing.

And then he saw Ermentrude.

She, too, lay still in the grass. He called to her, but she did not answer. When he got nearer, he too, cried out. Her belly and udder had been torn from her and all her life poured out on the ground.

He collapsed on the grass next to her, stroking her neck and rubbing her back. But she did not move and he did not think he could bear it.

"My sister!" he cried. "My friend!"

The ears that had listened to so much of his grief and loneliness could no longer hear him. He bowed his head over her and his tears fell on her wounds.

Oh, Lord Jesus, why did I not see the dogs until it was too late? And now, Your Ermentrude... Then words left him and he could only weep.

He felt the other goats press near. They all wailed, a chorus of poignant, piercing cries. He should lead them home. He should take them to safety. He needed to tend to their wounds. But he could not move.

"Fabrizio!" The voice called from across the hillside. Old Leonard and two of his helpers ran toward him.

"We heard the dogs, then we heard you and came as fast as we could." Old Leonard stopped still and planted his staff in the ground when he saw Ermentrude. "Oh, no, no," he said, shaking his head. "We came too late. I'm sorry, Fabrizio."

Fabrizio wiped the tears from his face and got to his feet. He picked up his staff and stood by Ermentrude. "I cannot leave her," he whispered, barely able to speak.

"Yet she is a heavy goat, better fed than you Franciscans. I don't think you can carry her either." Old Leonard pulled at his beard. "Let me take care of her for you. My boys can carry her back to my barn. She will not be left to the dogs. Why don't you and your herd come too? Come rest for a while."

"Thank you," Fabrizio said quietly. He bent quickly and tenderly kissed Ermentrude's head, while the men stood around silently watching. He did it, not caring what anyone thought, only wanting to honor his God-given friend. Then he rose and made the sign of the cross over her. Old Leonard removed his cap.

"For her life and her friendship, I thank You, Lord." Fabrizio could barely say the words, forcing his voice to remain steady. "For Your love for all Your creatures, I thank You, Lord."

He turned to the old man to thank him again, when he felt himself wrapped in a tight hug.

"I see yet again why your goats love you so much, Fabrizio. I will take care of her for you, for my good Franciscan."

"Could you take the meat to the nuns in town? They will

feed the poor with it. Ermentrude would like that. She always cared about the poor."

"I will do that, Fabrizio. I will do just that." Old Leonard gripped his shoulder. "You come now. You and your goats, come with me. My boys will bind her up and bring her along."

He nodded silently, then called to his flock in a low voice. "Come, Sancha. Come Lily. Bring your sisters. Let us go with our friend."

THEY MOVED SLOWLY across the hillside in funeral procession. Old Leonard in the lead with his hand firmly around Fabrizio's arm. The peasant's sons roped Ermentrude's body to a sturdy staff and carried it between them, each holding an end. All around them the goats mourned for their sister as they went. A ghastly, horrifying wailing that made people from Old Leonard's household come running to meet them.

Old Leonard led the herd into a large, airy shed, calling as he went. His words flew over Fabrizio's head, but the people around him responded. The peasant's servants drew water and brought bandages, oil, and herbs.

Someone brought a stool and Old Leonard urged him to sit on it. A woman appeared with a a cloth and bucket, took one of his arms and began to wash it gently. He blinked and recognized Celia, Old Leonard's wife. After a few moments, she looked up at him in surprise.

"You are not hurt?"

"The blood is from the goats, Celia," Old Leonard put in.

"The dogs attacked the goats and killed one of them. Brother Fabrizio fought a valiant battle. One of the dogs is dead too."

The words pulled Fabrizio out of his numbness. "I didn't kill the dog. Lily did. Where is Lily?"

He took a cloth from Celia and began to carefully wipe Lily, while Old Leonard himself worked on Sancha. Water for the washing. Oil and herbs after. And long cloth strips for the bigger wounds. The goats left off their wailing in the face of so much care.

All in all, the flock had done well against the dogs. One of the white ones would limp for awhile. Lily and Sancha had some deep scratches, but those should heal. Only Ermentrude would never recover. He looked around the shed, but did not see her. The men must have taken her to the place where they did their butchering. Fabrizio's stomach tightened.

"Celia, do you have any food and drink for our good brother here? We have missed the meal."

The woman stood up and wiped her hands. "The soup is still warm. When the friary bell rings, I put it on the table. But today the bell never rang, so after a while, we just had to eat. Let me stir the pot. Will you come in?" She looked at Fabrizio and then back to her husband, seemingly uncertain of what would be needed or done with a friar.

"We will come in." Old Leonard gave a decisive nod. "Look here, Fabrizio. Your goats are settling down to rest. They have all they need and my men will watch them. Let us go eat. Time for you to rest too."

Following Old Leonard, he entered the low kitchen and sat down near the end of a long rough-hewn table. The peasant took off his cap and rested it on his knee.

Large bowls of stew, bean and onion, were placed before them, along with several loaves of bread, each bigger than Fabrizio's hand. The food was delicious, and even though his stomach was upset, he tried to eat as much as he could in thanks for the kind hospitality. Somewhere out of sight a girl was singing a light, sweet song. Fabrizio found it strangely comforting.

"My granddaughter Maria," said Old Leonard, wiping his mouth. "She likes to sing while she works the loom. We should have some fine blankets ready for the winter. She has been singing very much of late."

"She has a beautiful voice," Fabrizio answered. "As clear as a bell." Then he thought about the friary bell. It did not ring? It always rang. But he did not want to tell his hostess she was mistaken.

Old Leonard was not a talkative eater, and Fabrizio was grateful for that. He was too weary to talk. But under the weariness, a small flame was kindling. A flame of anger. Anger at the cruelty of the dogs. Anger that Ermentrude had not had the horns to defend herself. Anger at himself for not being at her side to help her.

He glanced up once at Celia. She was stirring another pot over the fire, and at the same time smiled kindly at him.

"Would you like some more to drink, Brother Fabrizio? Would you like some more soup? We have plenty."

"I thank you, but no more. Your food is good, but my stomach is not right."

"He lost his favorite goat, Celia," Old Leonard said. "He lost his Ermentrude."

Celia looked stricken. "The goat the friars have had for so long? The goat that grew up with you?"

Old Leonard nodded his head. Fabrizio stared down at his bowl. He was afraid he would weep in front of his friends, and yet did not know why he was afraid. Celia already understood what Ermentrude meant to him.

That people, other than his own friary brothers, could know his life, have concern for his life, moved him. And surprised him. Yet there was Celia, wiping her eyes with her rough brown apron, just as if her friend had died and not his.

"Thank you, Celia," he said, strangely heartened.

He looked across the table at Old Leonard. "And thank you too, my friend. Thank you for coming to my aid."

"We are herdsmen, you and I. We watch out for each other." Old Leonard nodded his head as if it were as simple as that.

"I wish I had something to give you for your kindness to me and my flock."

Old Leonard shook his head. "No need, Fabrizio."

Celia's eyes lit up. "Would you pray a blessing on our house?"

He stood at the doorway of their home, made the sign of the cross, and prayed the Latin prayer for the blessing of houses. Then he prayed in their everyday language, asking God to pour out kindness on these friends in return for their kindness to him, asking blessing and strength on all their endeavors, asking for a good future for the songbird Maria and for young Leo who did so much to help the friary. Afterwards Celia kissed his cheek as if she had been his mother. Old Leonard gave him another gruff hug.

THE AFTERNOON PRESSED on toward evening as he and the goats came slowly down the mountain path, their steps faltering and unsure as they picked their way, every one of them aching for their sister who always took the lead. Lily took her place last in line where, more determined than ever, she kept her watchful eye.

He had not heard the bell ring for prayers. He knew from the angle of light and the feel of the air when the bell could be expected to ring, and somehow had missed the sound of it. Just as Celia had. It was like the loss of Ermentrude, the loss of something beloved and familiar, without which one stumbled forward into grayness.

As THE ROOF to the silent campanile came into view, Lily let out a warning bleat. A figure appeared on the path below them, head bent and climbing. After a few moments he recognized Kerstan. *Kerstan?*

Kerstan never climbed the hills. Kerstan spent his life in quiet rooms surrounded by thoughts and books, bursting out only to instruct scholars, or write letters for the Guardian, or to preach words that made hearts swell for the love of God. When Fabrizio waved, Kerstan stopped climbing and waited by the grassy hillock that marked the place where several paths met, until Fabrizio and his herd came near.

"Here, Fabrizio. Sit down. I must talk to you." Kerstan himself sank to the ground on the hillock.

At Fabrizio's command, the goats stayed near, lying or standing in the grass, unusually quiet. Exhausted, subdued, spent. He looked all around before sitting down himself to make sure there was no sign of dogs, then turned his attention to what Kerstan had come to say to him.

Instead of speaking, Kerstan covered his face and began to sob. Hard. Huge, gulping sobs.

Never in his life had Fabrizio seen tears in the tall scholar's eyes. Kerstan was one of the steady ones, imitating the Guardian in wise and patient counsel. Yet here he was almost choking over the sorrowful cries in his throat.

Fabrizio rested a hand on his shoulder while his thoughts spun rapidly in confusion. What had caused such sorrow? Was the Guardian ill? Then Kerstan would have pulled Fabrizio down the path and they would have rushed to their leader's bedside. No, he would not be ill. What else could be wrong? At last Kerstan's sobs quieted, and he drew in deep, shuddery drafts of air.

Fabrizio posed the question as gently as he could. "Did the talks between the Spirituals and the Dominicans not go well today?"

Kerstan rubbed his face on the sleeve of his robe. "There were no talks. Nobilus asked his two questions again. To each of them. 'Do you believe that Pope John has the power to establish precepts that govern the Franciscan order? Will you obey?' That's all."

"What did they say?" But even while he asked, Fabrizio already knew.

"Each one of them said no. From the youngest to the oldest."

Fabrizio said the words slowly, fearfully. "What happened then?"

Kerstan turned his red-eyed, swollen face to him. "They beat them, Fabrizio." His words came in short, gasping bursts.

"They tied the poor ones to trees. To posts. All around our square. And—and whipped them until the blood and flesh flew."

The words Kerstan had spoken were real, and yet not real. They hovered in a place in Fabrizio's mind, hovered like birds that could find no perch. An image of Sereno's thin fingers reaching to pet the goats came to him. "They do not have enough skin for the lash," he said quietly.

"They have even less now," said Kerstan.

The words that were not real circled Fabrizio's mind again, rushing his thoughts and flapping their wings, demanding entry, but he would not let them alight.

"What is happening to the friary, Kerstan? What is happening to our home?"

"I do not know, Fabrizio. I do not know."

They sat immobile as if the hillock were an island bound up in mountain fog from which no traveler dare set off alone.

Finally, Fabrizio took a deep breath. "Come," he said, standing up. The goats surged around him in response. But he had been speaking to Kerstan.

16

L eo stood outside the gates of the friary as they approached, a dazed look on his face. He took a few limping steps in one direction and then in another, seemingly uncertain of what to do or which way to go.

"He saw it," Kerstan said in a low voice to Fabrizio. "He was running an errand for Gustave and saw it."

Fabrizio could imagine what Leo felt. The moment when the familiar, understandable world was suddenly changed, and forever, by the discovery of great evil. How the air felt heavier, the birdsong turned to shrieks, and the sun itself cast gray light.

"Leo!" Fabrizio cried.

The boy turned toward the sound of his voice.

The task he would give Leo could help the boy. "Come with me," he said, taking the boy's arm and gently leading him toward the stables.

The goats eagerly sought the comfort of their home straw, but Sancha could not quiet and prowled the walls of the pen bleating pathetically, turning her head in every direction, looking for Ermentrude.

"Here, Leo," Fabrizio pointed. "Here is their fresh water and hay for their manger. There is the pitchfork. They have had a hard day in the hills and need comforting. Could you stay with them for me? I would stay myself, but I must go to my brothers right now."

The boy started to come to himself. He nodded. "I have helped my *nonno*. I like animals. I know what to do."

Fabrizio showed Leo the wounds on the goats, all while rubbing their muzzles, kissing their foreheads and doing all he could to show them his love. Then he put his hand on the boy's shoulder and looked intently into his eyes.

"God bless you for doing this, Leo. Many people destroy, but it is a gift to be a comforter. Do you understand? A gift."

Some of the light returned to the boy's eyes. Fabrizio patted him on the back, then reached out to rub Lily's muzzle one more time.

"Good girl," he said.

As he walked with Kerstan towards the kitchen, a distant flicker of black caught his eye. Titus was going into the chapel. Three other Dominicans spoke in French at the entrance to the stable, laughing at something Fabrizio could not comprehend. Two of the Dominicans' workers busily swept the steps outside the library doors. It was almost as though nothing had happened in the square.

Yet, a piece of rope hung tangled around a lower branch of the tree. Flies crowded around dark spatters in the dust.

Broken trails of dark blood were still visible along fresh troughs in the dirt as though heavy weights had been recently dragged away. The words Kerstan had uttered on the hillside fluttered loudly and more insistently in Fabrizio's mind, demanding a place to settle. But he would not give them one. He dared not.

Kerstan pushed the kitchen door open and they stepped inside. All the brothers were gathered there as if a council were underway. Gustave stood at his oak table, his arms crossed, hands strangely still. Emilian leaned on the table across from him. Benefice by the hearth. Both Quintus and Cantor were there. Was no one in the infirmary? Even Donatello was present, his lips pressed tightly together, face rigid, his distinctive blue mantle thrown over one arm as he paced back and forth across the back of the room.

The Guardian sat on a stool in their midst, surveying each member of his flock, watching closely with concern in his eyes, just as Fabrizio had done in the goat pen.

Emilian was speaking, a sharp, agitated tone in his voice. "There is historical precedence for scourging. It is of benefit in discipline." He spoke the words insistently, and yet, a high-pitched whine accompanied them, a note of begging.

Fabrizio looked around the room. No one nodded in agreement. Some faces wore the same dazed look Leo had worn out by the gate.

Kerstan raised his head. "The scourge is not a teacher," he said firmly. "It is a debater who cannot think of any more words to say."

"'Dull head, quick fist,'" threw in Cantor. "Right, Benefice?"

Emilian turned on Cantor. "What if the dull head belongs

to those who will not listen, who stubbornly cling to their own ways when all the Church is against them? They are the wrong-doers! They are the miscreants! Their rebellious spirits have asked for punishment. Tomorrow we may see good fruit from it."

No one answered him. Benefice looked troubled. He opened his mouth and then closed it again, as if suddenly aware that no platitude had the power to ease such distress.

Quintus spoke to the Guardian in a low voice. "I was allowed to wash him, but was forbidden to use herbs, either for soothing or healing. I fear for the rest of them too."

"They are supposed to feel their punishment," said Emilian. "The lash will finally get through to them." A desperate argument, but no one joined him.

Fabrizio could no longer turn from the truth of what had happened in the friary. The full meaning of it took roost in his mind at last. It alighted in a rush and he felt dizzy with the weight of it. His stomach sickened, and he shook his head slowly, like a drunken man, even as he felt his limbs tighten with anger.

"They will not change their minds," he said. "For them it would be like giving up Christ."

He stared across the room, not wanting to meet anyone's eyes. His gaze fell upon a round of cheese where it waited, forgotten for the moment, by the large cheese board. The board was made of solid oak. A farmer had crafted it from a tree on his farm and given it to the friary. Fabrizio glanced at the cheese again, then walked across the room toward it, his legs feeling stiff beneath him.

He reached for Gustave's sharp knife and began to cut the cheese into thick chunks. He set each chunk on the oak board, carefully and deliberately. One after the other, he cut and piled the pieces, until the cheese round grew smaller and smaller and at last disappeared. A tall mound of cheese filled the board. He lifted it with two hands and turned. In that heavy silence, all eyes were on him.

Emilian looked alarmed. "What are you doing with that, Fabrizio? Where are you going?"

Fabrizio ignored him and stepped toward the Guardian. "Dear Guardian, I am a Franciscan. I have taken the vows of Saint Francis. Vows of poverty, chastity, and obedience. My life has been planted on the words that God spoke to him, 'Give to the poor.' And now, I ask your blessing so that I may go feed the poor and starving among us."

The room had been silent. Now it became deathly still. Fabrizio gazed into the eyes of his Guardian, his whole heart in his look. The older man studied him in return, and Fabrizio saw that the Guardian understood the question beneath the question. And not only he, but all his brothers were waiting for the answer.

The Guardian took a deep breath. "This is a hard time for all of us. A time of confusion when it is hard to distinguish the fire of God from the fire of man's anger."

His voice was steady, thoughtful, as one working through a difficult problem, testing the words as he spoke them. "When confusion comes, we must turn to the foundational truths, the Scriptural truths, of our faith and our Order. They are the guideposts one after the other to help us find our way through the fog."

He had taken care to look at each one of the brothers in the small circle of the kitchen. His gaze came back to rest on

Fabrizio, and Fabrizio saw the decision being made in his eyes.

"Go." He nodded his head. "Feed the poor, Fabrizio."

Fabrizio bowed quickly then carried his cheese board to the door. Donatello swooped forward to open it for him, but Fabrizio went through it alone.

17

Fabrizio took the back stairs, the ones the Dominicans would be least likely to use. These led him directly to the three rooms at the end of the hall that had been set aside for the Spirituals. The stone rooms were sparely furnished like the rest of the dormitory. The first had only two small cots in it with small tables next to them. The men in the cots made no noise and appeared to be sleeping.

Fabrizio stepped in quietly and laid blocks of cheese on each small table. At his approach, one of the men started awake and pulled back at the sight of him.

Fabrizio could not miss the terror on the young face. "It is only me, Honorato, with some food for you."

Honorato blinked at him, his eyes smaller in a swollen face, then carefully lowered his head back onto the pillow.

In the next room, Venedictos was kneeling by his cot praying, his words soft, yet intensely spoken. Laudalino lay still, his angular face immobile, his eyes closed. Fabrizio stole in quietly, determined not to disturb either one of them as he left the food.

Knowingly or unknowingly, he came to Sereno's door last. His heart pounded as he put his shoulder against the door and slowly eased it open. He felt a pang of fear.

Sereno's bed was empty.

Palmer lay on his stomach on his cot, his body shaking with suppressed sobs. Fresh blood soaked through the blanket that covered his back, and Fabrizio felt the anger rise within him.

They had given Quintus orders not to heal. The pain of the wounds was meant to continue the punishment. Emilian sounded so sure the lash would bring about good results. Or, had Emilian been trying to convince himself along with the rest of them?

In these beds lay wounded, suffering Franciscans. Yet the friars had been told not to heal, not to feed, not to show compassion. What questions was the lash asking now—of all of them?

He wanted to rest his hand on Palmer's shoulder, to try to comfort him as he had tried to comfort Kerstan. But the weight of his hand would only bring more pain and Palmer had refused his sympathy before.

He piled the remaining cheese on each small table, again as quietly as he could.

Where was Sereno? Could the worst have happened? No, no. He must be in the infirmary. That could mean Sereno suffered more than any of the rest of them. Or perhaps he was better than the rest and had insisted on being the last attended. It must be that. He must be doing well if both

Quintus and Cantor felt they could leave the infirmary for a moment.

A voice stopped him in the hallway before he could reach the stairs. A loud, imperious voice. "What are you doing there?"

Fabrizio turned and looked down the hall. In the distance, Nobilus's black garments almost disappeared into the shadows, but his pale face stood out clearly, as if disembodied in the darkness.

The inquisitor strode forward. "Answer me! What are you doing?"

Fabrizio raised the board so Nobilus could see it. "I am the friar who has been given the responsibility of the cheese board. It is my humble duty here—"

Nobilus cut through his words. "Yes, yes, but what are you doing with it?"

"Fulfilling my vow to feed the poor," he stated clearly.

Nobilus glared at him. "You dare to enter these rooms and give the rebels food? After what I ordered?"

"Did not their fast end yesterday?" Fabrizio spoke as mildly as he could. "I have been all day with the goats in the hills and have only now returned."

The glare in the Dominican's eye lessened, but his words were still sharp. "Go, gather whatever food you brought, and take it back to the kitchen with you."

"No, sir," Fabrizio replied.

Nobilus took a step closer. "What did you say?"

Fabrizio did not move. The inquisitor was several inches taller than he, and easily looked to be a stronger man, but Fabrizio had his empty cheese board made from the cross-cut of an eighty-seven-year-old oak, grown in hills that had weathered many worse storms.

"I do not wish to be unkind or in any way disrespectful to any *guest* within the gates of San Stigliano—"

Manus was coming down the hall behind Nobilus.

"—but I cannot do what you ask."

"Cannot?" Nobilus bellowed, his voice ringing through the hallway. "Or *will* not!"

Fabrizio planted his feet and met the inquisitor's eye. "I am bound to vows as tightly as you are bound to yours," he said. "Therefore, I must say, *cannot*."

Nobilus' pale face reddened. "I have had my fill of rebels!" He raised his fist and plunged it toward Fabrizio's face.

It was a move that Fabrizio had seen too often in the years of his tough childhood, and his body remembered how to counter it without a thought. He swiftly raised the board, stepping toward the blow.

The oak held.

Nobilus stepped back with a roar of anger and pain. He swore an oath—one that would require great penance. Manus took a step toward him then stopped, glancing back and forth between the Dominican and the Franciscan. And for once looking uncertain.

Fabrizio did not move. Did not think of moving. He had wielded the cheese board against hunger just as he had wielded the ladle. He hoped the poor ones were eating quickly. But he desperately wanted to find Sereno, and the Dominican and his watcher were in the way.

Footsteps sounded in the hall behind him. "Is there trouble here?" came the Guardian's voice. Kerstan and

Donatello walked beside him, Donatello with all the strength of nobility in his stride.

"Yes, there is trouble!" Nobilus raised his injured hand. "Your friar is causing it!"

Kerstan's eyes widened and he glanced at Fabrizio with amazement.

"I will have him whipped like the rest of them!" Nobilus declared.

The Guardian rested his arm across Fabrizio's shoulders. "No, you will not. I have the authority over this friar. An authority given to me by the Minister General of the Franciscan Order and approved by the pope as the Vicar of Christ Himself.

"I have recognized the authority that you, Nobilus, have been given. You will recognize mine. No inquisitor can supplant the Guardian of any friary." These last words, though spoken in mild tones, sounded firm.

Nobilus tried to move his fingers and winced in pain. "Then you must discipline him!"

"For what offense?"

"He has dared interfere with what I am trying to do—by the authority of Cardinal Scantoni, with the approval of Pope John. And know this, Amadeus Walerian, I was chosen for this task because I do my work well. All the work I do for the Church of God is done well, and I will not let anyone hinder me."

In spite of this fiery speech, the Guardian's own voice remained calm. "Your actions recently have been somewhat confusing to all of us. Tell me, what is it you are trying to do?"

Nobilus stared at the Guardian as if he were an imbecilic child. "How can you not understand this? I am uniting the

Franciscan Order! I am purifying the Church of its disobedi-ence!" His words echoed long in the stone hallway until, their vibrations spent, they fell to the floor.

The Guardian did not flinch. He held the inquisitor's eye and waited to speak until all other sound had died away.

"By whose blood, Nobilus?" He asked it quietly, but his words pierced the air like a knife. "By whose blood?"

18

———

He found Sereno in the infirmary, face down on a cot. Quintus was bending over him. Fabrizio stepped forward, then hesitated as Quintus gently lifted the blood-stained sheet from Sereno's back.

It was not a human back. It resembled the sausages that Gustave boiled too long, the ones that burst their skins and clumped in sodden globs. Except—this was raw. And the smell was sickening. Fabrizio's stomach clenched and he turned away.

Cantor was laying out herbs on a table near the fire where small kettles of all shapes hung over the flames or tucked into the ashes. He beckoned Fabrizio over with a motion of his head then spoke quietly, leaning close to Fabrizio's ear.

"After the beatings, Quintus went outside to argue with the authorities, demanding to be allowed to treat the Spirituals. They ignored him and hauled them up to their beds. Except for this one. They seemed to think they might have overdone it, so they brought him here instead." Cantor shook his head and took a deep breath. "I have never seen Quintus so angry."

A voice broke through the hushed stillness of the room. "I must treat these wounds. I must keep pus from developing on them."

It was Quintus, but he was not talking to Fabrizio. Or to Cantor.

Then Fabrizio saw the Dominican sitting in the corner watching Quintus with an enforcing eye.

"No herbs," came the reply.

"Mustard, then," said Quintus firmly.

"Nothing but water."

"The water will not be clean enough."

The Dominican only shrugged.

Quintus gave a snort. "William of Saliceto," he said, in a carefully controlled voice, "who was the greatest surgeon at the University of Bologna, taught that pus is bad for a wound. All good doctors know they must keep pus from forming."

The Dominican remained unmoved.

The short, straggly white hair that ringed Quintus's head seemed to stand on end. His face reddened. "Look, you Frenchman!" he cried. "Bologna was pouring out knowledge throughout Europe, while your Paris was still trying to find itself. But I don't expect you to understand that. Hah! And you Dominicans think *Franciscans* are uneducated? I'm looking at the extent of your education right now, and it does not go far."

The Dominican's face darkened.

"I must keep pus from forming on his back." Quintus repeated his point, saying each word firmly, sharply, like the hammering of a nail. "And you will tell Nobilus that."

The Dominican stared back.

"You will tell him now!" said Quintus.

The man got to his feet, scowling.

As soon as the door shut behind him, Quintus nodded to Cantor who immediately started grinding away with mortar and pestle. The smell of sage rose into the air.

The aroma make Fabrizio think of a proverb that Benefice had once found for Quintus. *Cur moriatur homo cui salvia crescit in horto? Why should a man die who has sage growing in his garden?* It was a heartening thought.

"Warm the yarrow leaves, Cantor," said Quintus, studying Sereno's back. "I'll need the calendula lotion too—"

The door swung open. Another Dominican entered to replace the first, taking the same chair and watching with an even colder eye. Quintus, muttering under his breath, gently lowered the sheet and went to help Cantor.

Fabrizio picked up a stool and went to the far side of Sereno's cot, placing the stool so he could watch Sereno's face. The eyes were shut. Every line of the face rigid. The smell of the mutilated back even more sickening. Fabrizio had never seen such suffering, not even when his mother had died.

Sereno was not sleeping. Not resting. Sereno was enduring. Sereno was suffering so greatly for one thing only—to honor God by not being like Fabrizio. And this last hurt Fabrizio as much as anything else. He bowed his head and covered his face with his hands.

"Surely we are allowed to pray?" The words Quintus aimed at the Dominican were sarcastic. "Or will you dare block the words we say to God too?"

"I am not afraid of what God will answer," came the proud reply.

They may have spoken longer, but Fabrizio did not pay them heed. He opened his eyes and studied Sereno over the tips of his fingers.

Sereno.

The golden boy.

Healthy, brilliant, and strong.

Striding down the streets of their old town like all the world was his to examine, to marvel at, to enjoy.

Do you see that sign, Fabrizio?

Which one?

For the tailor?

He had looked dumbly around. This part of town was unfamiliar to him.

The red one, Fabrizio, with the picture of needle and thread underneath?

Yes, I see the red one.

Sereno had looked closely at him.

Do you know your letters? Only Sereno could say it in a way that was not insulting.

Some.

The ones for your name at least.

Sereno had guessed rightly.

Yes.

Then I will show you all the rest, Fabrizio, for a man should have all the letters he wishes at his disposal. It is good you have made a start. Very wise of you to have made such a start.

And Sereno had finished the job. He taught Fabrizio to read as they sat side by side on the stone bench in Sereno's garden. He argued daily with the cook, insisting the little hired boy take water breaks for lessons. Some nights the lessons continued by lantern light in the stables. On three different occasions, Fabrizio had been allowed in the great house itself.

His mother had been so proud. Every night as they made their beds in the straw by the goat pen door, he told her stories from the books he had read. She loved hearing them. As he told her of the fox jumping for the grapes that were just out of reach, her worn face relaxed into a smile. They would lie in their beds and stare at the roof beams, talking, wondering if the grapes had really been sour or sweet until their eyes closed in sleep.

The days went by and Fabrizio read more and more, hungry for words as he was hungry for food. With every book he mastered, he saw himself as more than just a little begging urchin. And hope grew in him.

Because of you, Sereno, I grew to read well enough to become a priest. But you are not proud of me now. Now you despise me. Oh, Sereno! If only we could agree like brothers!

He reached out to lay a hand on Sereno's head for prayer, but stopped before it touched the matted hair. Sereno had seen that same hand carrying a money tray and could not forget it. He would not want it touching him.

So Fabrizio put his hands together instead and spoke aloud the Latin prayer for the sick and wounded, and a prayer for those broken in heart. Then he prayed in his own language, not caring whether the scornful watcher understood or not. He prayed for Sereno's healing, for his heart, for his relationship with Christ. When his words were spent, he covered his face with his hands and wept silently into them.

A sudden commotion made him raise his head. Titus

stepped into the infirmary and spoke French in a commanding tone to the black-robed friar in the chair. The man nodded, got up, and left. But Titus did not sit down in his place. He stood near the door watching the other man leave, then after a few moments, shut it firmly.

"Use the herbs," he said to Quintus. "For healing, for soothing, to close the wound. Do all that you would do."

"Nobilus has given permission?" asked Quintus.

Titus did not answer the question. "Use the herbs."

Quintus studied his face for a moment, then motioned to Cantor. Cantor emptied his mortar into a pot of water that had been warming near the fire and stirred it with a long spoon.

"Fabrizio?"

He looked up, blinking.

"We will need to work on both sides of Sereno," Quintus said gently.

Fabrizio nodded, got to his feet, and moved aside. "I must check on Leo and the goats," he said. His voice did not sound like his own.

On his way out, he stopped by the fire where Cantor was working. "I must ask your forgiveness, Cantor."

Cantor's brow creased as he watched the pot, stirring constantly. "What for?"

"I lied to you. The day the Spirituals came, when you asked if I knew Sereno, I said I did not. But I knew him. Back when we were young boys. I should have told you then, but I was too afraid, too weak. Please, forgive me." He looked earnestly at his friend.

"You are forgiven, Fabrizio." Cantor rested his free hand on Fabrizio's arm. His tone was sincere.

"Thank you, Cantor. With all my heart, thank you."

"We will take good care of him, Fabrizio."

Fabrizio tried to answer, to convey what that meant to him, but found he could not speak. He bowed instead, and went out into the dusk.

NEVER BEFORE HAD the friars of San Stigliano neglected the tolling of the bell and the gathering for the Divine Office. And it wasn't neglect now. It was the horror of gathering to worship in the midst of shed blood, as if this day had been just like any other day in the rhythm of their lives.

The bell finally began to ring again at Compline. Fabrizio and all the brothers came to the chapel, except for Quintus who stayed in the infirmary. The Dominicans proudly filled their benches. The Franciscans warily filled theirs. As the chanting began, Venedictos walked slowly in, but he collapsed after a few moments, and Cantor and Benefice helped to carry him out.

19

———

The milking did not take long the next morning. The goats had little to give after their horrible day in the hills. There would not be much for cheese-making.

Gustave did not seem to notice. He was grinding chestnuts into flour, feeding the roasted, dried nuts into the quern, and turning the stone vigorously when Fabrizio brought the milk in. He stopped abruptly and wiped his hands on his apron. His mind was clearly on other things.

"I do not like this confusion, Fabrizio," Gustave whispered, though no one else was in the room. "How many do I cook for? Donatello says I must not waste so we can hire the workmen to start work on the chapel roof. Yet, I cook for people who do not come. Or, are for some reason not allowed to come. If I make less, everyone comes. The Dominicans already think poorly of San Stigliano because of the food. And the Dominicans talk to the pope! What do I do?" he said, raising his hands to the sky in question.

Fabrizio could not think. Could not offer any words. Had barely slept. He looked at the heavy stone and the mound of chestnuts, the sweat that already ran down the sides of the cook's face. "Where is your help today?"

Gustave rubbed his face roughly. "I told the boys not to come until tomorrow. In—in case the inquisitors do something else." Gustave did not have to explain. Fabrizio knew what he meant.

"Do you want me to take a message to Donatello? I know he is here already. His horse is in the stables. He can tell you what to do."

"Yes, thank you. Yes." Gustave reached for the milk bucket. "Ask Donatello."

Fabrizio stopped first at the infirmary. He glanced at the cots. Quintus was asleep on his own, the one he slept in whenever anyone needed him overnight. Sereno was still there, face down, head turned away, exactly as he had been when Fabrizio had left him the day before. No Dominicans were in sight. Cantor sat at the table by the fire looking sleepy.

"How is he?" Fabrizio whispered.

Cantor shook his head.

He knew that Kerstan always spent early hours working in the Guardian's study. Donatello, of course, must be there as well. He entered the library building and had not come far down the lamp-lit hallway when he heard the sound of voices engaged in intense discussion. The sound came from the

Guardian's study, and it was clear that Nobilus was in there with him.

The door had not been shut completely, but was open enough to give him a glimpse of a table corner. The back of a Dominican shoulder. The tight gray curls that fringed the Guardian's tonsure. There beyond, a swirl of blue cape.

He could not interrupt and at the same time could not get Donatello's attention without being seen. Sighing inwardly, he sat down on a stool in the hallway to wait. He tucked his hands into the sleeves of his robe to keep them warm, when with a start he realized he was not alone.

In the light of the oil lamps, he saw on another stool not ten feet away from him, the figure of Manus. Fabrizio bowed his head in greeting, but Manus did not acknowledge it. His eyes were on the doorway and Fabrizio saw paper and a pencil in his hand. Why was Manus listening so closely to the Guardian's conference? Was that the reason the door had been left partly open?

Fabrizio sat quietly and stared at the blank wall in front of him. He would never purposefully listen to counsel not meant for his ears. But with Manus writing down what was said? He held still and listened.

"It is reasonable to ask for some time to think," the Guardian was saying. "Isn't that what you wanted them to do? Think on what you have—what you have said?"

"They have had enough time," Nobilus answered in cool tones. "And we have already been here too long."

The sound of papers being shuffled on a desk top. "I have kept our *Custode* informed as usual of all that goes on in my convent. He understands that this could take much time."

"You may tell him that I am grateful for his understanding, but I will not give the disobedient more time to think."

A pause. More shuffling of paper.

"May I ask you something, Nobilus?" The Guardian's voice was gentle, thoughtful. "When Christ called you, did He woo your heart with His love or with threats?"

Fabrizio knew the sound of that voice well, the gentle questions that had led him out of his own anger, his own fears, words that poured gentle healing on the wounds of his soul.

Nobilus snorted and did not answer.

"If you will let me remind you—" the Guardian went on, but Nobilus stopped him.

"Do not presume to instruct me," he said in cold tones. "I am the one who will remind *you* of what is important. Obedience is what is important. Obedience to Christ and the Church. What I have told Venedictos, I think I must tell you too. You must obey the Church, because the Church does the will of God."

"Does it?" the Guardian asked quietly.

"Are you a madman?" The inquisitor's voice rose almost to a shout. "Yes!"

"Always?" The Guardian pressed his point. "Every moment? No errors? Are we not meant to test everything together? To search the Scriptures with the Holy Spirit in order to determine the truth of what is before us? Is that not what the Franciscan Chapter General does? Is that not why even the pope has advisors? You speak of obedience. Yes, but following one command of God does not give us the license to ignore the others. To use the violence of the world against fellow believers—"

A deep, dramatic breath interrupted him. A chair creaked furiously.

"Now you listen to me, Amadeus Walerian. From the time of Saint Francis onward, you Franciscans have been prone to extravagances in your theological understanding. You have not been grounded in good training like we Dominicans have been. This rigorist mania does not exist among the Dominicans. Therefore, I, as a representative of the pope and the cardinal, I will tell you what is the truth. I will tell you what you must obey."

Hostile silence filled the room. Fabrizio could feel it leak out the open doorway. When Nobilus spoke again, his tone was even colder. "I do not think you are fit to be the Guardian of this friary. Why, yesterday you did not gather for worship at the required hours. Do you do only what you wish to do in the moment? You act like a rebel yourself. A rebel who would keep me from doing what I have been appointed to do."

Fabrizio's heart raced. *What was going on?*

"I am a rebel?" Frustration filled the Guardian's voice. "We have done everything you asked! We have even stood by while you were brutal to these poor ones! May God forgive us!"

Manus wrote swiftly on the paper in his lap.

"You ask that God forgive you?" Nobilus sounded stunned. "For obedience to the Church?"

"Yes," the Guardian spoke firmly. "Obedience to some things is a sin against God."

Nobilus uttered a cry. "I refuse to talk about this with you! I will not talk with you anymore!"

The sound of a chair being forcibly shoved back made Fabrizio leap to his feet. Nobilus emerged from the study and without even a glance at him, strode off down the hallway. One of his hands was heavily bandaged. Manus got up and followed him like a shadow.

The door to the study had been left wide open. The Guardian's face was in his hands as he leaned on his desk. Kerstan sat motionless staring blindly at whatever work lay on his own. Fabrizio caught Donatello's eye and beckoned.

Donatello joined him in the hall, shutting the door behind him. "Did you hear?" he whispered.

"Yes," Fabrizio answered. "And so did Manus."

Donatello raised his eyebrows.

Fabrizio opened his mouth to say more, but no words came. He kept thinking of Nobilus accusing the Guardian. After a few moments, Donatello asked, "What do you need?"

Fabrizio told him about Gustave's concern over the amount of food he should prepare, and his fears.

Donatello shook his head and sighed. "I know, I know. Tell him I will come talk to him sometime today. Tell him not to worry. Whatever he can do will be the best. The problem may be solved soon anyway." He glanced down the empty corridor, in the direction the inquisitor had taken. "I do not think the Dominicans will be here much longer."

MIDDAY QUINTUS REPORTED that Sereno was at last truly sleeping. The Dominicans had withdrawn for some urgent council of their own, and Quintus had used their absence to coat Sereno's back with every needed herb before they returned.

The suffering and exhaustion of the infirmary and dormitory disheartened the whole friary. The thought of the violence done inside their walls oppressed the Franciscans into silence. The brothers did not talk with each other at their midday meal or when passing each other on the way to their various duties. And with the Dominicans appearing everywhere and at any moment, they did not even dare to gather in the kitchen to talk.

How deeply the community felt this oppression was seen when the Guardian sent Emilian and Benefice to town carrying cheese rounds, rye loaves, and a large basket of eggs, along with a message for the small group of nuns there. Fabrizio met the two on the road when his goats were returning from the lower pastures.

Emilian told him of the Guardian's request, that the nuns would tend the poor for them and pray for the townsfolk while the Franciscans worked through this crisis. They all shook their heads in grief at the words.

Never in all the years the friary had been in existence had they ever turned the poor and needy elsewhere.

Fabrizio spent much of his time with the goats, bathing the wounds the dogs had inflicted, pasturing them nearby, and giving them scraps that the Spirituals were either too sick to eat or not permitted to eat; he wasn't sure which. He missed the open companionship of his own brothers. He feared for Sereno. He grieved for Ermentrude.

In the privacy of the goat pen he took sanctuary, speaking quietly but freely to Sancha and Lily and the others. He patted Sancha's flank now as she rubbed against his robe. They were both missing Ermentrude and Fabrizio felt the need to talk, just talk. Sancha had listening eyes. And she did not want to leave his side.

"People are confusing, Sancha, have you noticed that? Do I confuse you sometimes?" He looked deep into her golden eyes.

"No, I don't think I do. And I am not flattering myself when I say that. I am Fabrizio the Franciscan as I have been for all of your life. Can you tell by the color of my robe?

"I can tell a Dominican from a Franciscan. But do the robes mean as much as we think they do? If I put on a black robe, would I forget who I am? If Sereno put on my robe, would he be as horrified as if I put on a black one? Are our robes too short? Are our robes too long? Is Christ fooled by robes?"

The talk had been half silly. Fabrizio felt as if he were rattling nonsense. An unexpected sob caught at his throat. Sancha looked at him earnestly.

He took a deep breath, stroked her smooth back, and tried to resume the lightheartedness. "Ah, Sancha. You know who you are. You are a goat. And yet, why are you a goat and not a sheep? You don't fare very well in Scripture you know. You end up on the wrong side.

"You don't want to be on the left side of the Almighty God. You know why you end up there? Because when Christ came to you in the sick, the imprisoned, the poor, you did not recognize Him..."

His hand fell from the goat's back. His voice trailed off in horror as the full meaning of that passage smote him.

Christ. Had he failed to see the Lord Jesus Christ?

Was it truly Christ in the face of each of these Spirituals —sick, imprisoned, and poor as they were— just as in the face of his brothers?

Look for Christ, the Guardian had said. And he had.

He had seen Him, yet missed Him. Had often turned his heart from Him.

He slid to his knees, heart pounding. "My Lord God, forgive me! I—I did not see You! You in them! But they are wrong and You are never wrong!

"I am confused. I do not know what to do. Or even what to think or feel." Tears leaked out from his closed eyes and dripped into the straw. "Speak, Lord, what will You say to me? What do I do?"

Fabrizio waited, listening. Aching. He heard the goats complaining to each other as they pushed for their places in the straw. He heard a horse neigh and snort. French voices in the distance. A night bird croaked, and the wind rattled the door of the goat pen.

But there was no familiar voice in his heart. No gathering of Scriptures in his mind. No comfort from the Holy Spirit of God who resided within him.

God was utterly, devastatingly, silent.

20

———

At the sound of the Compline bell, his tongue stumbled through its prayers. Afterwards he climbed the dormitory stairs to his room at the far end of the hall from the Spirituals. He laid down on his bed facing the wall. He felt hollow and bereft as he had never felt since his childhood, and it was terrifying.

Kerstan and Emilian came in tired and distracted. They said a sentence of blessing to each other as they did every night. Then they too laid down on their cots. Kerstan blew the last candle out and cold darkness filled the room. Fabrizio stared into the dark until, hours later, sleep finally came.

～

THE SOUND of a voice roused him. He sat up instantly and looked around, fully alert. Emilian's deep, full-bodied snore rumbled and snapped in the dark of the room. The night wind blustered against the windowpane.

The voice came again, a voice as loving and firm as the Guardian's. It was asking him a question.

When is God silent, Fabrizio?

Fabrizio turned his head from side to side, wondering how to see this speaker so he could address him properly. "I —I do not know."

When He has already spoken.

"What is it, Lord?" he whispered. "What have You said? You wrote so many things, and I only know a hundred. Help me please, God. Help me!"

Frantically he searched his memory. The Gospels? The Epistles? Where to start? Romans? Everything in the friary had been wrapped around the book of Romans lately. He would start there. What was the Romans verse?

He spoke quietly, carefully, trying to make sure of each word while his heart pounded. "If we have been united with Him like this in His death, we will certainly also be united with Him in His resurrection..."

What unites My people, Fabrizio? What joins them to me? Something they have done or something I have done?

"Something You have done." He thought he answered rightly, but he could not be sure. And he felt so dull.

What unites My people, Fabrizio?

He thought of the passage again. "Your death, Lord. Your resurrection."

Kerstan coughed in his sleep and rolled over. The wood frame of the cot squeaked.

Am I divided?

"No," Fabrizio whispered.

His heart went to the verse from his favorite book —Ephesians. The Guardian had read it every day at meals the week before the Spirituals arrived. And the Ephesians verse was one that had been assigned to everyone in the friary. Even Gustave and the launderers knew it, because it contained an important point for brothers who lived under the same roof.

"Make every effort to keep the unity of the Spirit through the bond of peace," he whispered, then waited, longing to hear that loving voice again.

Whose unity is it, Fabrizio?

"Your Spirit's, Lord."

It is not waiting for man to agree. It is already there.

He repeated the verse to himself, over and over again, whispering it carefully in the dark, treasuring the words as if he had gold on his tongue, while his mind pored over them.

Keep the unity—not create it—*keep it*, because it is something Christ has already done.

Anguish rose up in Fabrizio's heart as he thought of the events and feelings of the last weeks. He got out of bed and knelt on the cold floor. "Forgive me, my Lord Christ! My heart has divided Your church! I have despised my brothers. I have turned away so I would not even have to see them or talk to them. I have been so angry with Sereno. Oh, Lord, I am so sorry. I am so sorry. What You have done, I have worked to undo. Forgive me!" Over and over, he pleaded. "Forgive me!"

Come, Fabrizio. Stand up.

It was a gentle, familiar command. Like a goatherd calling his goats.

Fabrizio got to his feet.

As the voice spoke, the room slowly filled with light. Light like the sun and yet not from the sun, but like the radiance of a rich man's jewel when sunlight catches it unexpectedly in the middle of a summer day.

I want you to see what I see. What I have done.

For this is true.

The brightness increased.

It was as if the stars of the sky had entered the small room. In astonishment, Fabrizio saw where the light was coming from. Emilian had become a sparkling jewel, glowing with beautiful rosy brilliance, even as he slept in the humble cot. Fabrizio looked to the far end of the room and there Kerstan too gleamed like starshine.

Fabrizio held up his own arms and saw light radiating from them. "How—how?" he whispered, unable to finish the question.

What you see does not come from you. It cannot come from any man. What you see is My righteousness. This is what My death, My resurrection, has given to all My people.

Light filled the friary. It poured out of the wood-framed doorways and down the halls. Then the walls of the friary melted away into the night and Fabrizio saw the town at the bottom of the hill. Humble Armonia, it too was aglow.

Light came across the mountain tops and from the far side of the sea—a light so beautiful and joyous that he wept for the delight of it. He turned slowly, stupefied with wonder in the midst of all the radiance, trying to take it all in.

He heard singing, the sound of many voices that could not contain their happiness. The sound was not coming from the people of the light, but from somewhere else. He turned around again, wishing he could see the singers, wishing beyond everything he could see the speaker of the voice, but he could not.

"This is marvelous! Marvelous!" he cried. Then he held still so he could hear every note of the song.

The words were in a language he could not understand, but what they sang of, he knew. He had heard it in the Scriptures he had memorized and the ones that were read at mealtimes and chanted at prayers. He had heard it in the hymn the Guardian had sung over his mother's grave.

Now the song fell around him even as it filled him. He fell to his knees and bowed his head. For Christ Himself, Love Itself, was the song.

Love was the voice that had awoken him in the night. Love that poured out like an extravagant mountain waterfall. He felt the enormity of it as it filled the land, and the town, and the friary, and the room, while Emilian snored and Kerstan slept.

He knelt by his cot, his heart full of praise, and remembered the words the voice had said.

This is true.

21

He raised his head and saw that he was just where the vision had left him, kneeling by his cot on the stone floor. Emilian had already lit the candle and was sitting up, stretching his arms. Kerstan yawned loudly from the corner.

Fabrizio crawled onto his cot and rubbed the stiffness from his knees. He stared at his companions as if he had never seen them before. Behind the beard and stubble, the tonsured heads and sleepy eyes, the light of Christ's righteousness glowed unseen.

How could he tell them? How could he begin to explain what he had seen in the night? They needed to know, but would they think he was crazy?

Suddenly, Kerstan climbed out of his bed and peered out the window at the lightening sky. "It must be later than I thought," he said. He pulled on his robe and headed for the door in the same motion. "I must finish packing the new books. Prentice and the scholars will take them to Milan today."

"And today is my day to draw water. I am going to teach my class in town since the boys cannot come here," Emilian said, as he too reached for the door. "I'll get water for your goats once I've drawn some for Gustave."

Humble people doing the practical duty that lay before them, but Fabrizio knew what the grace of God had made them.

He walked to the goat pen in a dreamlike state, still filled with the glory of the night's vision. Just before he entered the pen he paused to look up at the morning stars. "You made us look like them," he said out loud with quiet awe. "Your righteousness is far beyond my poor words. Thank You. Thank You."

He took his time milking the goats, singing to each one, calling them by name as he milked them, thanking them for the milk which helped the friary so much. As he was starting on Lily, he heard sounds in the stables next door.

Doors opened and closed. Voices whispered. Between the creak and clank of harness and gear, he heard the squeaking groan of a carriage being wakened from its rest and pulled into the courtyard. It would be Prentice and the scholars preparing to leave for Milan.

Fabrizio stayed in the goat pen, singing softly, not wanting to get in the way of those who had such an urgent errand. When he had finished the milking, he set the pails on a safe shelf out of the goats' reach and picked up the pitchfork. As he thrust the fork into the hay and swung it into the long rough manger, he was suddenly aware who he wanted to tell about the vision first.

Sereno. He wanted to tell Sereno.

Another quarter of an hour passed before he heard the creaking he was waiting for—the large friary gates grating open, the rumble of rolling wheels, the sharp thud of horse hooves, increasing then slowly fading. The scraping of the gates closing again.

Fabrizio put down his pitchfork, picked up the milk pails, and crossed the now empty square. He would give the milk to Gustave and hurry to the infirmary.

The sky lightened over the eastern hills. No clouds appeared. The morning was clear and chill with the promise of sunshine to come. A good day to be in the hills.

Friars crowded the kitchen when Fabrizio entered with the milk. The Guardian himself was there, a piece of paper in his hands, along with Donatello and Kerstan. Emilian and Benefice too. Fabrizio remembered how they glowed in the vision and he couldn't keep the smile of joy from his face. But why had both Quintus and Cantor left the infirmary again? Fabrizio poured the milk into Gustave's large kettle then turned to face them all.

Kerstan spoke first. "We waited for you, Fabrizio. The Guardian has received special instructions for today. We can begin to speak of them now."

"We found them nailed to the chapel door," Donatello put in. Fabrizio met his gaze. They both remembered the last talk between Nobilus and the Guardian.

"Do you know the Dominicans have gone?" Donatello added.

"The Dominicans?" Fabrizio felt confused. "The noise in the stables, that wasn't the scholars?"

"Not yet," Kerstan replied.

"The Dominicans took the Spirituals with them," said Cantor flatly.

Fabrizio stared at him and then looked questioningly at Quintus. "All the Spirituals?"

Quintus nodded sadly. "He could barely put his feet to the floor when they carried him out."

Fabrizio felt panic spring to life in him. "Where have they gone?"

The Guardian spoke at last, concern and sorrow in his eyes. "I do not know. I would guess to Florence where Cardinal Scantoni has gone now. No doubt to prison."

Fabrizio thought again of Sereno's torn back. "The cardinal could not wait for them to heal?"

"Nobilus was in a great hurry this morning," said Donatello, but the tone of his voice said that he thought the inquisitor's behavior strange.

"And these are our instructions," said the Guardian. They all turned to him, ready to listen.

"'The friars of San Stigliano are to stay inside the walls of the convent today. You may not set foot outside until tomorrow morning. You are to observe the Divine Office without fail and spend the day in prayer.'" He looked up at them. "It carries the seal of the pope's authority."

The Guardian glanced quickly at Fabrizio. "No fasting, just prayer."

"I can fast now," said Fabrizio.

The Guardian's glance lingered on him a moment, a curious look in it.

"I do not understand this," said Kerstan. "Stay sequestered? We are not monks. We are friars!"

"It seems Nobilus has forgotten this," said Cantor.

Emilian burst out, "We need a day of prayer. Yes. But today I am teaching a class on shoemaking to the boys in town. They are expecting me today. They need to earn money to eat. Antonio has donated the waste rope to make sandals. This means a future for them. I must be faithful to what I have promised."

"We will have to send them a message with anyone who comes to see us," said the Guardian. "Or Donatello could take it down."

Emilian frowned.

Fabrizio said nothing, but his heart sank. He would not be able to tell Sereno about the vision after all. He had imagined talking with him throughout the day, whenever he could, and coming again in the evening after the goats were asleep. He would have taken Quintus' place on the watcher's cot, grateful for the chance to be able to take care of his brother all night.

But now Sereno was gone to Florence. Ill as he was, suffering as he was, they had put him in a coach and taken him to Florence. Never to return.

Fabrizio felt hollow inside. The sense of loss overwhelmed him. He had just recognized his brother's face and now his brother was gone.

THE KITCHEN BOYS ARRIVED, sleepy, but ready to work. Benefice and the silent server left to ring the bell for prayer. Fabrizio went with the others to the benches in the chapel.

In the midst of the familiar chanting, the vision of the night came back to him, lifting his spirits. Here they sat, gray-robed friars in a bare, leaky chapel, but now he knew they were receivers of incomprehensible love. And so were Sereno and his friends. How had they all missed it?

In every psalm, he saw love. In every Scripture reading, he saw love. He was seeing Christ, as God and the Guardian had wanted him to. Now he understood what the Guardian had said to him weeks ago in the infirmary. That the Gospel was so great he would spend his life trying to understand it.

Halfway through the service, a restless ache began to take hold of him. A discordant feeling after the wonders of the vision. He could not understand this ache or quell it, no matter how much he placed his mind in the chant.

He found later that the goats too, were unusually restless. The pen jostled with surging bodies leaping about, not caring who was around them. Lily tore at the edge of the feed box, making deep grooves with her teeth. When an impatiently shaken head drove horn tips into another's flank, a chorus of bleating filled the air.

"It is not even time for midmorning prayer yet, and you are already behaving this way?" cried Fabrizio. "How will you make it through this day?"

He washed the wounded goat with the water Emilian had drawn for him, but the agitation in the pen did not subside. Sancha put her head against his knee and bleated loudly again and again.

The goats wanted—needed—to get up into the hills. Yet they had been ordered—by a man who did not understand goats, *and* who no longer was present—to stay in the convent.

What if he took the goats up into the hills today anyway? How could that hurt anything or anyone? He loved to pray in the hills. It would still be a day of prayer for him. Besides, the friary needed the cheese from these goats. The poor needed the cheese. And the taste of the cheese was in those hills.

Should he ask the Guardian? He paused to think. If the Guardian said yes, the Dominicans and their cardinal would punish him. They had accused him for nothing already. Fabrizio could not face bringing trouble on the Guardian. The Guardian meant too much to him. No, better to risk his own punishment at the hands of the Guardian, than risk the Guardian's punishment, or even removal, at the hands of others.

He waited until Benefice rang the bell for prayer, then watched through the slats of the door as, across the square, the friars entered the chapel again. When he heard the faint sound of chanting, he picked up his staff.

The goats pushed around him eagerly as he opened the door. They crossed their corner of the square to the small door by the closed gate. Fabrizio unlocked the door and cracked it open, looking far down the road. No coaches or horsemen could be seen.

"Come, sisters. To the hills."

The goats hurried through the door and Fabrizio, with his hand on the doorframe, took a last look at the friary courtyard. It was empty but for the old oak with its long, bent limbs and drying leaves. Between the branches he could see the windows, dark and silent, where the Spirituals had once been. He thought of all the days he had longed for them to leave, for life to return to the happiness it had been before they came. He could see no happiness returning now.

Had there been something that they were all meant to do? A particular purpose from God—far higher than the motives of any church authority—that had brought the Spirituals and the San Stigliano friars together for this time? Had they missed it, just as he had missed seeing Christ?

Sancha gave a questioning bleat and gently nudged his knee. He took a deep breath, closed the door firmly, gripped his staff, and made ready for the climb.

THE SMELL of smoke came on the air. The peasant farmers had more fields to burn before the winter came. He thought of Old Leonard and how much he hated that practice of burning. Soon it would be over, because there must be time to plant the fields again before the freezing cold.

As they approached the hillock, Sancha turned toward the familiar path, the one that led to their favorite grazing areas, but he called her back.

"No, my friend, I cannot bear to go that way yet." His heart still grieved for Ermentrude. He did not want to see the place where she had been killed.

"Come. We will take this new path," he said, striding ahead of them in the other direction. "The trees are not as thick, but I think you will find food well enough."

As he climbed the path with the flock, Fabrizio knew he had decided rightly. The animals, glad to be out, had already calmed, trotting up the hills. At the crest of the first one, they rested.

He found a good place to sit while the goats milled and grazed around him. He bowed his head and prayed for Sereno. He asked forgiveness of God for both of them, for their hardness of heart, for their blindness. He asked God for strength and healing for Sereno in the ordeal with Cardinal

Scantoni. And most of all, he thanked God that Sereno was his brother.

The wind shifted, bringing with it a stronger scent of smoke, but there was something in the smell that was not of plant and earth. The goats began to bawl and cluster together nervously.

Fabrizio stood up and he could smell it even more. A disturbing odor. There, he could see it now. Smoke rose from over the crest of the next hill to the south. The fire producing it seemed to be growing, and he felt alarm. Didn't the road to Milan lie in that direction? Was it someone's farm? Someone's house? Had Old Leonard's fears of the autumn fires come true?

The restless ache he had fought down in the chapel sprang to life in him again. He could not stay still. He picked up his staff.

"Stay here, Sancha. Stay here all of you. I have to see this." The goats would want to stay together. And, he wouldn't be gone long. He could gather them again quickly enough if they strayed a little.

He walked in the direction of the smoke, down the slope of this hill, then up the pathless side of the next, climbing over scrub grass and stones. At the crest, he looked down, bewildered. Sure enough, the road lay along the base of the hill below. Along it were three coaches in a line, three coaches parked carefully away from the burning field, for a large portion of the hillside was indeed on fire.

Several wagons paused on the road to see the sight, but he paid no attention to the people in them. Or to the workers who moved in and out, tending the flames. His eye had been caught by those who stood in a group, watching the fires in this strange field.

They were black-robed friars. With familiar faces. And wasn't that Manus walking near the fires, pointing and shouting to the workers?

All in a rush he realized what he was seeing.

Six fires had been lit in the field, each one billowing with smoke. In the middle of each fire stood a post.

And tied to each post, a man.

22

He stumbled partway down the hill and ran the rest of the way. He crossed the road and hurtled into the midst of the fires, looking frantically for Sereno. The flames ate at the legs of the poor ones, leaping eagerly at their thin robes, then climbing higher.

Honorato began to scream. Palmer choked on terrible sobs. Venedictos hung as still as a statue.

Fabrizio darted between the fires like a goat gone mad, tugging wood away from each, one here, one there, until he reached Sereno.

Sereno wore the same look of intense suffering as in the infirmary. Head drooping, silent. A Dominican stood nearby watching him.

Fabrizio dove past the watcher, grabbed one of the logs under Sereno and dragged it away from the fire. "No!" he cried, "No! Sereno! Sereno, my brother! Oh, God in heaven!"

He pulled another log from the fire. The watcher did nothing to stop him. It was Titus.

Titus did not move. His face was covered in tears. His expression like one already dead.

Fabrizio bent into the fierce heat, his fingers grappling for a hold on the wood, when a shove pushed him down. He scrambled to his feet, and knocked the man who reached for him to the ground.

He looked up again into Sereno's face. The eyes had opened. "Peace, Sereno!" he cried out. "Peace, my brother! Forgive me!" He wrenched more wood off the fire, desperate to break up the flames.

A voice sounded above him. Weak, anguished, struggling to speak. "Peace, Fabrizio...Forgive...me."

He looked up into Sereno's pain-filled eyes and for a fleeting moment Fabrizio saw the light of the vision between them.

"Sereno, my brother!" he cried. He had rejected Sereno as brother before; he could not say the word enough now.

The executioner's servants fell on him. Two, then three of them, grabbing him at once. He was full of fury and fought as he had fought the dogs before. But three, now four strong men were too much for him.

They hauled him up, carried him across the road, and threw him down into the ditch on the other side. Others built the fire under Sereno again. Fabrizio scrambled up and scurried between them toward the flames. But they grabbed at him, cursing, and threw him harder and farther.

Some watchers just stood and laughed at him, this crazy friar taking on so many men. But he could not stop trying to put the fire out. He could not keep from calling out, "Sereno!" no matter what they did.

He plunged up the hill once more. Before they could grab

him again, a sudden whoosh of flame and sharp crack of wood made everyone stop to look. Flames completely engulfed the young Honorato. Honorato...and Sereno.

Fabrizio could not see Sereno through the fire and smoke. He fell to his knees coughing, choking, and crying out. *Domine miserere! Domine miserere! Lord, have mercy!*

Someone grabbed his arm. Before he could struggle, he heard Titus's voice in his ear. Eyes stared into his own. Amber eyes, like Sancha's.

"Fabrizio, you cannot save them! I could not save them. I tried. Before God, I tried! They are in the hands of the civic authorities now. But I can save you. I have called them off, but you must go now, before they seek to arrest you."

Titus pulled Fabrizio to his feet and helped him down the hill, away from the fires and the executioners, before releasing his arm. Fabrizio limped painfully across the road, breathing heavily. Smoke stung his eyes and everywhere around him the bitter smell of his brothers' death filled the air.

He climbed the other hill slowly. At the top he turned to look back. Another post burst into full flame. Venedictos.

A small movement between the posts caught Fabrizio's eye. A worker found the staff he had dropped. The man picked up the staff and threw it on the fire. For a moment, Fabrizio couldn't breathe. Then a great sob shook him.

Domine miserere, he whispered over and over, staggering half-blind in the direction of his goats, sobbing as he went.

HE ENTERED the friary through the door by the gate and

slowly, numbly, began to lead the goats toward the stables. From somewhere, he heard Emilian's voice raised in indignant accusation.

"Fabrizio!" Then closer, questioning. "Fabrizio?"

Fabrizio forgot the goats and sank to his knees in the square. He bent until his head was in the dust.

Again and again he saw the columns of fire. Again and again he saw the flames take Sereno. Whether his eyes were open or closed, he saw the same. His stomach writhed and he retched into the dirt.

"Get Quintus! Get Cantor, hurry!" Emilian's voice was calling out to someone.

Fabrizio rocked on his hands and knees, head down. Sounds of voices and running feet broke into his misery. Quintus was on his knees at his side looking closely at him. Cantor wiped his mouth with a rag. Kerstan and the Guardian bent over him.

"You are injured, my son," said the Guardian.

"His hands are burned," said Quintus. "And he is bleeding. Look at his neck. His face! What happened to you, Fabrizio? Who did this?"

Fabrizio did not answer. Instead he raised his head and looked around. "Do you smell that?"

"The farmers are burning the stubble in their fields," said Benefice, in a voice meant to calm. "It's the last of the harvest, Fabrizio. *Esto laborator, et erit Deus auxiliator.* Be a laborer and—"

"No!" Fabrizio cried. "That is no harvest! Those are the fires of hell!"

His eyes found Kerstan. And the Guardian.

"They're burning them. They are burning every last Spiritual on that hill!"

Eyes widened. Mouths dropped open. Faces froze still as stone as they stared at him.

"This can't be," a voice whispered. Benefice again. "It—it wouldn't happen."

Donatello broke from the group and ran toward the stables for his horse. "Get my horse!" he shouted to his groom as he ran. "Open the gates! I must see this!"

Emilian hurried to the gates and shoved the locking bar aside, swinging one side open for Donatello. After a few moments, Donatello emerged from the stables, his horse already speeding to a gallop. Then he was through the gate, his mantle flapping around him.

The friars clustered around Fabrizio again.

"But what happened to you, Fabrizio?" the Guardian asked.

"I tried to put out the fires. I tried to stop them. But I couldn't." He sank back onto his haunches, his voice low. "And all that my brother would have said to me, would have been to me, I have lost."

"You—you tried to put out the fires?" Emilian sounded stunned.

Fabrizio raised his head slowly. "I saw Sereno just before the flames took him. Do you know what he said?" He stared at each face around him, wanting each of them to see what he had seen. To hear what he had heard.

"He said, 'Peace, Fabrizio.'"

A violent sob caught in his throat. He tried to get up. Cantor held out his arm to help, and Fabrizio leaned on him.

Blood dripped into his eyes. Fabrizio wiped it angrily

away. "What will the Lord of Hosts say to us when he returns? *You killed My precious ones? Because you did not agree on what you should wear or how you should live, you killed My sons?*"

"My Guardian," said Quintus quietly, "I must get him to the infirmary. Those burns—"

"Wait. He is not ready," the Guardian whispered.

The sound of horse hooves in full gallop came from the road. All fell silent watching the gate for Donatello's return. In a few minutes, he rode into the square, his horse breathing hard. They looked up at him anxiously.

"It is just as Fabrizio said." Donatello dismounted, his face ashen. "Terrible!" He shook his head vigorously, as if trying to shake the image from his mind.

"And there is more. When I got my horse, I saw that some of the wood for our roof is missing. I suspect it too is burning. And, Emilian, your rope is gone."

Emilian started. "They took the rope? They can't do that! It was given to the poor! They used our rope! They..." His voice broke off. The anger fled from his face as a new horror took hold. "They have made us murderers." He covered his face with his hands.

Kerstan took a long, careful breath and let it out slowly. "I confess." He spoke reluctantly. "I have hated these Spirituals and all the trouble they have caused us. Was I not a murderer in my heart already? Our Lord said that in Matthew's Gospel, didn't He?"

"I, too," whispered Emilian, from behind his hands.

Benefice crossed himself and stared at the ground.

The memory of the vision came back to Fabrizio, that voice of Love, the way the light filled each one of them, the joy of the song that flowed through the night. "We started from the wrong place," he said quietly.

"What do you mean, the wrong place?" Kerstan asked. "How the wrong place?"

"We began with the things that divided us. We drew attention to what the Spirituals hated about us and what we hated about them. They made the same mistake too. And those points were argued over and over."

Emilian frowned, but it was his thinking frown, and no impatience was in it. "You mean, we should have studied what we had in common, the things we agreed on. We should have started there?"

Kerstan broke in. "But we did start there! At least, Titus and Sereno tried to. That day they led the talks and made Nobilus uncomfortable."

Fabrizio shook his head. "No. I do not mean that. We should have started with something more solid and sure than common opinions, or practices, or convictions. We should have started with the surest thing of all. With what Christ has done."

They watched him closely, all these dearly loved faces. All his brothers. How precious they were!

He continued on, trying to put the truth of the vision into carefully chosen words.

"Christ united us with Himself in His death. In His resurrection. And so we *are* united.

"That unity—with Christ Jesus Himself—is what joins us to our brothers. It is a bond more sure and solid than the rising and setting of the sun. *Far* stronger and truer than any custom or practice. And superior to all of them."

He took a deep breath. "We should have started with

Christ."

A small breeze scattered dry leaves around the courtyard, bringing with it wisps of the nightmarish smoke. Fabrizio shuddered.

Cantor spoke gently. "We must bathe your hands, Fabrizio."

He nodded in reply. He could no longer ignore the burning, aching wounds. But he had something else to do first.

He slid his feet out of his sandals, bent to the ground painfully, still half leaning on Cantor, and picked them up. Gasps came from the watchers as Fabrizio stood barefoot in the dust. They knew what his action meant.

He held the rope sandals Emilian had made sole-to-sole in his burned and bloodied hands. He did not dare think of the loneliness that lay ahead of him; he only knew of the path he must take.

"My Guardian, in your humility we all call you brother, but you are the only father I have ever known," Fabrizio said. "A wise and loving father. But I must give these to you now. I will always be true to my Franciscan vows, but I can no longer be a convent friar." He held the shoes out, searching his Guardian's face, hoping, pleading, for understanding.

The Guardian did not speak, but waited. Listening.

"You told me to look for Christ and I did." Fabrizio could barely get the words out. "I saw Him burning over the hill."

He pushed the sandals again toward the Guardian. "Please," he whispered. "Please, I cannot keep these."

The Guardian looked intently at him, but Fabrizio could not understand the meaning of the look.

"Please," he whispered one more time.

The Guardian did not answer. Instead he bent down and

slowly, deliberately, slid the rope sandals off his feet, first one, then the other, until he too, was standing barefoot in the dirt. He straightened and held the sandals sole-to-sole in his hands, just as Fabrizio held his.

Fabrizio stared at him. *What did this mean?*

Kerstan bent to the ground. And Emilian. Quintus and Cantor and Benefice. Brother after brother took off their sandals until all feet were bare. Fabrizio stood in the middle of them all, head bowed, weeping.

AN HOUR PASSED, and more, in which Quintus and Cantor bathed and wrapped Fabrizio's wounds, while Fabrizio at last told them and the rest of his brothers about the magnificent vision. And as they listened the light of the truth filled their hearts and eyes.

It was an hour in which the Guardian penned a final missive to the *Custode*, and Kerstan and Prentice reviewed the procedures for delivering the Book of Romans to the Visconti in Milan.

Cantor gathered herbs to use in healing those they might meet. Benefice said goodbye to the chickens and gave his flute to the small silent server, the one he had taught to ring the bell. Emilian cut the lowest foot of length from their robes to give to the poor, and collected the sandals to give to his class of shoemakers. Fabrizio gave instructions to Leo about the goats.

"You're a good lad," he said as the goats nuzzled the boy's knees. "Look, they've already claimed you. They remember how well you cared for them when they were sad and sore. "

Gustave, their lay brother, wept and packed sacks of food for them, bread and cheese, apples and boiled eggs. "I know some say you are not to carry sacks, but please take these for the first day. Come whenever you are hungry," he said. "I will feed you. I will always feed you."

When the time had come, seven poor friars, in shortened robes and bare feet, walked out of the Friary of San Stigliano while Gustave sobbed openly and the tall Donatello shed dignified, noble tears. They walked up and over the hills to where the last of the fires still smoldered, to where Nobilus was addressing the crowd that had gathered at the burning, and where Manus was directing the men digging a pit.

In the crowd, Fabrizio saw Old Leonard's cap and his son's great shoulders. He saw the rich man who wanted a wife for his son and the poor man who wanted work. He saw the gray-haired man with a cane, his arm around his daughter. He saw Antonio, the one who led all the peasants in burning the fields. Nobilus was telling them, the friars' own people, about the disobedient rigorists.

"Do you see how the wrath of God burns? How He is right in His judgments?" Nobilus trumpeted in triumph, waving his arm in the direction of the grisly posts.

One by one the friars of San Stigliano crossed the road and made their way through the listening crowd to the ashes of their brothers. Ignoring the speaker, they knelt and crossed themselves, and dipping their fingers in the warm embers, traced the sign of the cross on their foreheads.

Nobilus, struck silent, stared at them. Then he found his voice again. "What are you *doing*? What *are* you doing?"

As they rubbed the ashes onto their arms, he yelled again. "You can't do this! By heaven, you can't do this! Amadeus

Walerian, you were to stay in your convent. Disobedient rebels! I'll come after you next!"

The friars didn't listen, and the townspeople weren't listening any more. They moved away from the Dominicans and toward their own friars, reaching out their hands to those they knew best, wanting to understand, and believing that those who had prayed so faithfully for them were the ones who spoke the truth.

Old Leonard and Antonio broke away from the crowd and mounted the hill to get ashes for their foreheads too. Several others followed. More, and then more, bent to cross themselves with ash-coated fingers, while Nobilus bellowed into the wind.

The seven poor friars walked through the crowd, blessing their people as they passed, and took the road that led between the hills toward the town. Fabrizio touched the ashes on his forehead and heard again, *Peace, Fabrizio.*

"Peace, Sereno," he whispered, as tears filled his eyes.

He felt a nudge at his side and looked down to see Sancha next to him.

"Are you sure? I won't have scraps for you anymore." Fabrizio wiped his eyes with his bandaged hand and looked at the hills around them. "But the Lord will provide for you."

In the distance, they heard the bell of San Stigliano ring the hour. It didn't sound as boldly as when Benefice pulled at the rope, but the silent server was doing his best.

The seven poor friars lifted up their heads as they walked and began to sing.

Soli Deo Gloria

AUTHOR'S NOTE

Some of the questions that naturally arise while reading historical fiction are these: Which parts of the story come from historical reality and which come from the fictional story alone? Or, which are "real" and which are "not real?"

On May 7, 1318, four Spiritual friars were burned to death at Marseille. The entire Franciscan Order, both Conventuals (convent friars) and Spirituals, was horrified.

For the sake of this story, I have changed the number and the month of the burnings, and have moved the event to a location in Lombardy, approximately 253 miles to the northeast.

My friars—both those in the convent of San Stigliano and the Spirituals—are fictitious characters. The tensions that tore at the Franciscan Order were very real, and I worked to present them, in the guise of character thought and action, as accurately as I could. The events Kerstan mentions in Chapter Four did, in fact, happen. And inquisitors, both Franciscan and Dominican, "disciplined" erring friars. In 1318, the inquisitor was actually a Franciscan. I chose to use a Dominican in order to be able to reveal other aspects of the historical climate, and to help keep characters distinct in the minds of the reader.

The Friary of San Stigliano and the town of Armonia are the only fictitious geographical locations. All others mentioned are real. The papacy was in fact located in Avignon (present-day France) and not in Rome at the beginning of the fourteenth century. Bologna did indeed have its university before Paris did, as Quintus asserts.

William of Saliceto was truly a surgeon at the University of Bologna. The popes mentioned—Celestine V and John XXII—were also historical figures. I tried to present the attitudes and actions of Pope John XXII true to history, even though he, naturally, would not have issued any specific orders for the fictitious friary of San Stigliano.

I spent hours researching medieval medicine and plant lore, but Quintus begs you to remember that the study of medicine has grown far beyond the understanding of his day, and to consult your own doctor rather than using his remedies. Quintus always believed in keeping up to date on medical knowledge.

I made every effort not to attribute something to the Lord God that He has not said or done. Every portion of Fabrizio's vision was taken from throughout Scripture.

Division in the Christian Church, as the ages attest, is very real. So is the unbearably great pain this division causes —to the individual Christians involved, to the church at large, and to the world.

But equally true is that unity in the church is completely based on what Jesus Christ has done. And the staggering reality is that by faith in Jesus Christ, we *are* united with Him. Therefore, being divided from each other is a metaphysical impossibility. The disagreements we have, and must honestly deal with, assume vastly different shapes when we realize this.

For those interested in reading more on these topics, here are the main sources I used.

The History of the Franciscan Order: From Its Origins to the Year 1517, by John Moorman.

Franciscan Poverty, by Malcolm D. Lambert.

Keepers of the Keys: A History of the Popes from St. Peter to John Paul II, by Sir Nicolas Cheetham.

Holy Bible: New International Version, especially John 17; Romans 6:1-5; I Corinthians 1:10-13; Ephesians 4:1-6; and Philippians 2:1-4.

Note: The friars of San Stigliano do not refer to specific numbered verses of Scripture, because at that time the Bible had been divided into chapter sections only.

Also, Lambert disagrees with Moorman and Cheetham on various points, and it must be assumed that they disagree with him on those same points.

ACKNOWLEDGMENTS

To the following people, my deepest, heartfelt thanks:

My test readers: Caleb Eckhardt, Bonita Krupp, Dorothy Woodbury, Sue Zelt, Laura Eckhardt, Hannah Olson, and Bjorn Olson. You graciously brought your life and reader experience to the manuscript and saved me from a host of errors.

Josh Eckhardt for connecting me to Meghan Kern and her knowledge of the smell of medieval ink. And to Aaron Mueller for some quick Latin checks and other phrasing. All errors are mine alone.

My family: Dale, Kristen, Jenn, and Adrienne, for all the years you willingly listened, read, and encouraged me while this story took shape in my heart and mind.

My graphic designer Kristen Langefeld. There couldn't be a better designer to work with on the planet.

My daughter Jenn, for being the first, last, and always

reader. You are the writing colleague other writers can only dream of. Thank you, thank you, thank you!

My husband Dale, (and the rest of my family) for your amazing and overwhelming love and support when a series of brain injuries almost ended everything. And for letting Fabrizio's story move you so much.

Dr. Neil Munhofen, for staunchly pulling me out of the pit of post-concussion syndrome and getting my life back for me.

Dr. Corey Osborne, for patiently and cheerfully cutting through the mire of PTSD that followed, so Fabrizio and I could both tell our stories.

To those who prayed either for the writer or this book when things got rough. Your concern and your prayers kept me going.

To the one and only living God and the Lord Jesus Christ, for life, love, redemption, forgiveness, healing, and all things good. All honor forever.

ABOUT THE AUTHOR

Rhonda Chandler was born in California and spent her childhood traveling with her family in Asia Minor, Europe, and all across the United States. In 1979, she graduated from Concordia College, Nebraska (now Concordia University) with degrees in education and history.

After teaching at the high school level for several years, she left in order to devote her time to her husband and daughters, and to writing.

She now lives in southern Illinois with her family where on Saturday mornings they make breakfast, brew coffee, and talk for hours about all the important things in life.

Rhonda also writes contemporary fiction and fantasy fiction, both with spiritual and historical overtones. To find out what's new, visit her at rhondachandler.com and subscribe to her mailing list.

If you enjoyed this book and found it valuable, please leave a review on Goodreads and on Amazon, Kobo, or wherever else you purchased it. In today's world, reviews are very important in helping people like you find this book. Thank you so much.